"Do you need me to spell it out, Maggie?"

Landon's lips creased into a smirk. He grabbed her hand and brought it to his mouth. His lips traced the ridge of her knuckles. "I wanted to get into the good graces of my lady boss."

A blaze ignited in her stomach. Much like the one he'd created in the dark interior of his truck when he'd slanted his mouth over hers in a searing kiss.

"Landon, I don't…"

A storm of fury and lust flared in his eyes. Her heart seized in her chest. Before it jumped back to life again, the emotion in those dark depths vanished.

He lifted his mouth from her hand. "Liar."

Dear Reader,

I'm a big believer in "do-overs"—where would we be without second chances? From sports to elections to falling in love, everyone deserves another try at getting it right and winning their heart's desire.

Landon Cartwright and Maggie Stevens are two people who are in desperate need of a second chance, even if they can't see it. Both of them need to let go of the past and realize love can be a part of their lives again, but boy, can they be stubborn about it! As someone who also found it difficult to take another chance on love (but the gamble paid off!), I just knew these two were perfect for each other. While Maggie is in a better place to take that sometimes frightening leap into the unknown, poor Landon really needs a few nudges from Maggie and her entire family to realize that a second chance is just what a certain cowboy needs.

I hope you enjoy Landon and Maggie's story!

Christyne

THE COWBOY'S SECOND CHANCE

CHRISTYNE BUTLER

SPECIAL EDITION®

Published by Silhouette Books

America's Publisher of Contemporary Romance

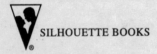 SILHOUETTE BOOKS

ISBN-13: 978-0-373-65462-8

Recycling programs
for this product may
not exist in your area.

THE COWBOY'S SECOND CHANCE

Copyright © 2009 by Christyne Butilier

All rights reserved. Except for use in any review, the reproduction or utilization of this work in whole or in part in any form by any electronic, mechanical or other means, now known or hereafter invented, including xerography, photocopying and recording, or in any information storage or retrieval system, is forbidden without the written permission of the editorial office, Silhouette Books, 233 Broadway, New York, NY 10279 U.S.A.

This is a work of fiction. Names, characters, places and incidents are either the product of the author's imagination or are used fictitiously, and any resemblance to actual persons, living or dead, business establishments, events or locales is entirely coincidental.

This edition published by arrangement with Harlequin Books S.A.

® and TM are trademarks of Harlequin Books S.A., used under license. Trademarks indicated with ® are registered in the United States Patent and Trademark Office, the Canadian Trade Marks Office and in other countries.

Visit Silhouette Books at www.eHarlequin.com

Printed in U.S.A.

Books by Christyne Butler

Silhouette Special Edition

The Cowboy's Second Chance #1980

CHRISTYNE BUTLER

fell in love with romance novels while serving in the United States Navy and started writing her own stories six years ago. She considers selling to Silhouette Special Edition a dream come true and enjoys writing contemporary romances full of life, love, a hint of laughter and perhaps a dash of danger, too. And there has to be a happily-ever-after or she's just not satisfied.

She lives with her family in central Massachusetts and loves to hear from her readers at chris@christynebutler.com. Visit her Web site at www.christynebutler.com.

Dedicated to my own Nana B…Margaret Elizabeth Blakeslee,
and my aunt, Carol Ann Baranowski,
both of whom continue to live on in my heart.
And to my mother, Sandra Jean Toms,
thank you for your love and strength!

Extra special thanks to Charles and Gail for your belief in me,
"The Goddesses" at WriteRomance—Alison, Christina,
Jen, Sandi and Tina, NHRWA and everyone at the
eHarlequin boards for all your support!

Chapter One

"You no-good, rotten thief!" Maggie Stevens stomped across the trampled grass of the fairgrounds and tried not to spill the frothy beer from the plastic cups she held in her hands. "You're stealing my man!"

Kyle Greeley shot her a sardonic grin and continued to peel bills from the large roll of money. By the time Maggie reached him he'd handed over at least a hundred dollars to the cowboy standing next to him—*her* cowboy.

"Not man, babe," Kyle said. "Men."

"What do you mean, 'men'?"

She shot a look at Spence Wilson, one of the hired hands who'd worked for her for the last few months. Then she saw Charlie Bain step from the shadows, his gaze locked on his boots.

She should've known.

While spending a beautiful summer day enjoying Destiny, Wyoming's, Fourth of July Celebration with her daughter and grandmother, she'd seen neither hide nor hair of her cowboys.

Until now.

"It's nothin' personal, Miz Stevens," Spence said. "We enjoy workin' at the Crescent Moon, but Mr. Greeley's pay is too good to pass up."

Maggie fumed. The dangling carrot of more pay had charmed away ranch hands—at least her young and strong ones—once again. They took the bait like a pair of hungry rabbits.

You did, too, at one time.

Okay, so a few candlelight dinners wasn't cold, hard cash, but she'd been enamored all the same by Kyle's smooth-talking ways. Then she'd found out what a scumbag he really was.

Kyle leaned into her. "You know, Maggie, you could be quite comfortable if you'd accept my offer for your land. Buy yourself a place in town, spend more time with your daughter, get yourself a man…"

She glanced at the beer, trying to control her anger and the urge to dump the liquid over his head. She gritted her teeth. "I've told you before, my land isn't for sale."

Movement caught her eye, and she saw her former employees scurry into the shadows of the darkened barns and empty animal corrals.

Cowards.

She looked back at Kyle. "Why stop with those two? Why not wipe me out completely and go after Willie and Hank, too?"

"Those old coots should've been put out to pasture years ago." He stepped closer, wrapping a finger around a strand of hair that had worked loose from her ponytail. "Admit it, you can't handle all that land, cattle and horses."

Maggie jerked her chin, freeing his hold. "Go to hell, Kyle."

She headed for the bright lights of the raised wooden platform beyond a cluster of cottonwoods. He fell into step beside her.

"I remember a time when you didn't want me to stay away."

She shook her head, barely able to tolerate that she'd once been taken in by his baby-blue eyes, chiseled cheekbones and charming lies. "Three months," she said. "Three months of romancing me to get my land."

He smirked. "Sometimes a man's got to make sacrifices. I never could figure what Alan saw in you. Then I realized he'd stuck around to get his hands on your ranch."

She spun to him, furious. "Well, he didn't. And you can forget about getting your hands on it, too."

They'd reached the trees. Kyle leaned in and grabbed her arms. Whiskey laced his breath. She mentally kicked herself for not noticing sooner. Sober, Kyle was annoying, but after a few drinks, he could get downright mean.

"I can put my hands any damn place I please," he said.

A flash of a buried memory caused Maggie's stomach to lurch. Beer splashed over the edges of the cups and dripped over her fingers. "You bastard," she choked. "Take your hands off me."

"Not until I'm good and ready."

A flicker of panic coursed through her, but anger snuffed it out. "Get ready now or you're going to find yourself with a face full of Budweiser."

"You wouldn't dare—"

With an angry flick of her wrist, she launched the contents of the cups at him. He jumped back, releasing her with a shove. "Goddammit!"

The liquid splashed on Kyle's fancy, snap-button shirt and her sundress, leaving enough for round two. "Don't dare me anything." A step backwards took her deeper into the trees. "Back off."

Greeley seized her again, his blunt nails digging into her arms. "You're gonna pay—"

"She told you to leave her alone."

Maggie froze as a low, commanding voice rumbled over her shoulder.

Actually, it came more from over the top of her head. She was acutely conscious of a man towering behind her. Overwhelming her. The husky tone causing a ripple of…what? Need? Awareness?

Annoyance crossed Kyle's face. "This is none of your business, Cartwright."

"Maybe not, but the lady's made her feelings quite clear."

"Let *me* be clear." Kyle took a step closer, his attention focused over Maggie's head as his hands tightened on her. "If you want to keep your job, I suggest you turn and walk away."

The man behind her took a step closer. "Let. Her. Go." His voice grew harder with each word.

Kyle flicked his gaze back to Maggie. "We still got business between us." He dropped his hands and stepped back. "Don't bother showing up at the Triple G tonight, Cartwright. In fact, I suggest you leave Destiny. For good."

Spinning around, Greeley vanished into the darkness.

Oh, boy, that was…she wasn't sure what that was, other than Kyle being his usual idiotic self. A deep breath helped. Maggie turned to thank her rescuer, but her foot caught on a tree root, and she stumbled backwards.

A pair of strong hands clamped her waist, pulling her back against a solid chest and rock-hard thighs. The man's jaw brushed her hair, a rush of hot breath flowed over her ear.

Twisting in his grasp, she tipped her head back to look at his face. Intense eyes stared at her from beneath the crown of a black Stetson. Dark stubble outlined his mouth and covered his jaw. A shiver she couldn't control raced through her. He dropped his hands and took a step back.

Maggie struggled to speak. "Thank you…for, well, thank you."

"No problem." He tucked in his chin, effectively blocking her attempt to peer further under the wide brim of his hat. "You okay?"

"Y-yes." She nodded. "I'm fine."

"You better get going before he decides to come back."

Before she could reply, her rescuer stepped around her and followed Kyle into the darkness. She watched his tall form disappear, trying to ignore the sudden rush of butterflies zooming around her stomach. Placing the blame for them firmly on Greeley, she glanced at what remained of the beer. Racy and Leeann were waiting for her. She'd better get moving. Mindful of the tree roots, she headed toward the crowded dance area.

Maggie offered a few hellos to familiar faces before she caught sight of her best friend in the middle of the dance floor with her seventy-year-old ranch hand. Willie tried his best to keep pace with Racy, who was four decades his junior, but like everyone else, he was distracted by her flame-red curls and undulating curves.

The dance ended and Racy joined Maggie. "Boy, Willie can still do a mean two-step." She grabbed one of the cups. "About time you got here. Where've you been? And what happened to my beer?"

Maggie poured the remains of her drink into Racy's. "I got sidetracked."

"Doing what?"

Maggie ignored the question, renewing her determination not to let Kyle Greeley's antics spoil her fun. "Where's Leeann? I thought she was meeting us."

"Her beeper chirped about ten minutes ago."

"I thought Gage gave her the night off."

"Yeah, well, being a deputy in a small town means you're always on call. Besides, you know Sheriff Steele," Racy snorted. "All work and no play makes for a pain-in-the—"

Maggie cut her off, tired of her friend's nasty comments about the local lawman. "High school's long gone, Racy. Let it go."

"I have!"

Maggie raised an eyebrow.

Racy flushed. "Let's not waste time on ancient history. Where's your grandmother and Anna?"

"Nana B. went back to the ranch after collecting her blue ribbons, and Anna's sleeping over at a friend's house."

Racy's face lit up with a bright smile. "So, you're a swinging single tonight. Honey, let's find someone to push that swing!"

Flashes of denim, tanned skin and a black cowboy hat filled Maggie's head. It'd been dark among the trees, but she easily recalled broad shoulders, shirtsleeves rolled tight against strong forearms and long legs encased in snug jeans.

Maggie pushed away the details and focused on her friend. "Don't you ever give up? I told you, I'm not interested. And unless you've forgotten, I've got a few things on my mind. Especially now. Greeley walked off with Spence and Charlie tonight."

"Those low-down, belly-crawlin' snakes! And you thought they had staying power. What are you going to do now?"

What was she going to do? She needed help. Hopefully the ads she'd placed all over town would bring in some fresh faces. "The same thing I've been doing all along," she replied, "keep on keeping on."

"Well, not tonight. Tonight is for fun and what you need is a red-hot cowboy who'll leave you too sore to move and too tired to care."

"What I need is to get home. I've got a pile of paperwork waiting and—"

"Oh, come on. It's a holiday!" Racy finished the last of the beer and tossed the cup in the nearby trash. "We're celebrating our country's independence, not to mention our own. Besides, the place is swarming with hunky cowboys."

"Forget it, I'm not interested."

"Look, I'm gonna find me a dance partner and I suggest you do the same. Then another and another." She offered a quick wink. "Personally, I'm shooting for double digits."

Maggie watched as Racy latched onto the closest cowboy and led him onto the dance floor.

"How long does it take to reach zero?" she muttered.

* * *

Zero.

Those were his chances of getting another job in this dot-on-the-map town called Destiny. Great place for an out-of-luck cowboy like him.

Landon walked across the teeming fairgrounds. The sun had set, and clusters of teenagers and families enjoyed the game booths and carnival rides that twirled in bright splashes of neon color.

He sidestepped an excited little girl carrying a prized stuffed animal and a breath-stealing squeeze compressed his chest. Shoving a hand deep into his pocket, his fingers curled around a familiar oval object. His boots shuffled to a stop and he closed his eyes against the memory before it had a chance to bring him to his knees.

It took a long moment, but he succeeded. Breathing deep, he opened his eyes and spotted the sheriff chatting with a group of men. Giving a tug on his Stetson, Landon pulled it lower on his brow. If there was anything he'd learned in the last few months, it was that the law was best avoided.

Hunger gnawed at his belly as he ducked into the food aisle, but he ignored the battling aromas of fried hot dogs and spun candy. The fifty dollars tucked in his pocket would have to last until he was employed again. After standing up for that lady, he was hell and gone from his next possible job three hundred miles away.

But what a lady.

Honey-colored hair and a sweet, fresh scent. Despite a shapeless dress, he could attest, thanks to having her body pressed to his, she had curves in all the right places. He hadn't meant to get so close, but the weight of her body against his and the feel of her hair catching on his whiskers stayed with him.

Then she'd looked at him. A flash of something—longing,

maybe—came through the anger and fear. A warning bell had gone off inside his head.

Leave. Now.

He'd ignored his own advice long enough to make sure she was okay, then followed his former boss to make sure the jerk didn't come back.

Damn, he needed a job.

Greeley's ranch was the largest in the area. The man meant it when he told him to get out of town. Big ranches and their owners carried a lot of power in small communities.

Landon headed to the far end of the parking lot where he'd left his truck and horse trailer. The dark shadows and relative quiet were the most he could offer his best friend right now. Hell, G.W. was his only friend, and the main reason for pulling off the highway earlier today.

"Hey, boy," he said as he stepped inside the trailer and moved beside the stallion. "How's the leg?"

He crouched down, murmuring softly as he ran his hands along G.W.'s forelimb, checking the area around the shipping boot. The horse snorted softly and shifted away.

"I know you hate these things, but it should help with the swelling."

It wasn't.

Landon had first noticed the horse favoring his leg the night he'd been not-so-politely told to leave his last job. Being on the road the last seven days meant he'd done a piss-poor job of icing the injury. He needed to find a place for the two of them to bunk down for a while, so he could take care of G.W. properly.

Three jobs since his release, three times told to move on.

He'd been foolish enough to reveal his conviction the first time. Never again. Now he did his best to keep to himself, but somehow the news always got out.

His stomach growled again. He opened the chest in the corner and found it empty. The ice packs were only slightly cool.

He leaned his head against the side of his horse. "I'm going to grab some chow and another bag of ice. Be back in a few."

He stroked a hand over G.W.'s smooth coat, then exited and locked the trailer, heading toward the market across the street. Bright fluorescent lights shone on a woman behind the counter when he entered.

Was that wariness on her face?

He offered a quick, polite nod then walked to the first aisle. Five minutes later, he'd moved back to the cashier when a dog-eared piece of paper on a bulletin board caught his attention. The words "Wanted: Cowboys" jumped out at him.

Damn, he must be crazy.

He yanked the paper off the board and shoved it into his pocket. After paying for his stuff, he crossed the road back to the parking lot with a sandwich, a cold soda and a bag of ice. He peeled back the plastic wrapping around the day-old bread with his teeth. It was stale, but he hoped it would cover the bad taste in his mouth left by the store clerk's apprehension.

His hair was too long and he was a week away from his last shave. Maybe that's all it was. Or maybe it was because he was a stranger in a small town. She'd beamed at the two clean-cut cowboys with pressed snap-buttoned shirts and shiny belt buckles who'd come up behind him, obviously knowing them.

Landon shrugged off his mood and finished the sandwich in two bites. He wasn't usually filled with his own thoughts. Not since his release. Before, he'd had plenty of time to think. Now he preferred a hard day's work that left him too tired for anything but sleep. Something he hadn't done much of over the last week.

He moved to the back of the trailer and led G.W. outside, taking the boot off and crushing ice around the injury. Standing in the light from an overhead parking lamp, he opened the soda and took a long draw on it, then yanked the piece of paper out of his jeans pocket and looked at it again.

"Okay, Crescent Moon, you're my last chance."

A soft shuffle invaded his consciousness, then sudden pain exploded between his shoulder blades. Seconds later, he smashed headfirst into his trailer.

Maggie waved goodbye to Racy from across the dance floor. She ignored her friend's answering frown and made her way through the crowd. Unable to find Willie, she gave up and decided to head home alone.

Gave up looking for her cowboy rescuer, too.

"No, not *my* cowboy," Maggie muttered, digging her keys from her purse.

Guilt settled in the pit of her stomach. She'd heard Kyle warn the stranger not to show up for work. She hated the idea he was now jobless because of her.

Offering him a job at the Moon had occurred to her while she stood on the sidelines of the dance floor. She needed a man—heck, she needed men, and as many as she could afford.

Kyle's words came floating back to her.

"Buy yourself a place in town, spend more time with your daughter, get yourself a man."

Nope. Not that kind of man. She didn't have the time, strength or the emotional energy to deal with that.

Not anymore.

Heading across the full parking lot, she checked her watch. Almost ten o'clock. With her daughter gone and her grandmother probably tucked in bed with a book, she'd have plenty of time to attack the mess on her desk.

Exactly what she wanted to do on a hot summer's night.

The promised relief of an overnight thunderstorm hadn't materialized, leaving the air sultry and thick. No, what she'd love to do was head home to enjoy a long dip in the cool waters of the pond behind the house.

Minus a bathing suit. And wouldn't it be nice if she wasn't alone.

The image of a certain cowboy drifted into her mind. This time Maggie let the fantasy play out, smiling at their sensual image. "Okay, girl, admit it, maybe Racy's right. Maybe it's been too long—"

A high, shrill neigh filled the air, startling her. Maggie froze, heart racing.

The second time the horse cried out she knew it was scared to death. The commotion was coming from the end of the row of cars. She raced toward it and saw a honey-colored stallion tethered to a trailer, its eyes wide with panic. The animal was frantically trying to free itself. She reached out to calm it, but stopped when she saw three men fighting not ten feet away.

Actually, it was more like two bullies beating up the third, but he fought back, twisting and kicking, despite being held by both arms. A fist crashed into his face and the man sagged.

Maggie gasped. "Stop! Leave him alone!"

The two creeps looked at her, breathing hard. Stetsons shadowed their faces. They released the beaten man and took off into the dark. The man crumpled.

She rushed to where he lay face down in the dirt. "Are you all right?"

He groaned and pressed large hands against the ground. The muscles across the wide expanse of his shoulders tightened beneath his shirt as he attempted to get up.

"That was a dumb question. Of course you're not all right." Maggie's fingers hovered between his shoulder blades, inches from long strands of hair covering his collar. "Don't move. I'll get help."

"No," he said, low and determined.

Maggie dropped to her knees. She wrapped a hand around his upper arm to steady him, her fingers small in comparison to his muscular bicep. Heat radiated from his body into the humid summer evening.

"You're hurt. Please, let me—"

"No." His refusal left no room for argument. "That's the last thing I need."

A zing of awareness raced through her.

The cowboy twisted and rolled onto his back. A cloud of dust rose as his head lolled to the side, away from her. A string of curses followed another moan. Dark hair fell across his forehead and blood trickled from the corner of his mouth.

She grabbed her purse and pulled out a handkerchief. "Look, I don't know why you and your buddies got into a fight—"

"They're not my buddies," he muttered.

"Then we need to call the sheriff." Forced to lean over him to press her hankie to his mouth, her fingers scraped the whiskers on his jaw. It reminded her of the dry stacks of summer grass in her barn. "Did they steal something from you?"

"No. I did a good deed and got my ass kicked for it," he growled through clenched teeth as he pushed himself up on one elbow. "Typical, always doing the right kind of…"

His voice faded as he turned toward her to shove her hand away. Two black eyes, one swollen shut, collided with hers. Steely fingers clamped around her wrist.

"You."

Chapter Two

"You!" Maggie echoed, her heart pounding in her throat.

His fingers seared her skin and she tugged free. He grabbed at her handkerchief, held it against his mouth. His denim shirt, ripped open to his waist, was covered in dirt and spatters of blood. A black Stetson sat on the ground nearby.

"Ohmigod, this wasn't—" She hadn't recognized the other men as they scuffled in the dirt, but now…Greeley's foremen. "They jumped you because of me."

"No." Looking away, he wiped at the blood on his mouth.

"I don't believe you."

He rolled onto his hip, one leg bent at the knee, and gave his head a quick shake as if trying to clear it. "I don't care what you believe," he rasped, pushing unsteadily to his feet. "Where's my hat?"

Maggie rose, ready to catch him if he fell. She grabbed the dusty Stetson, and held it out to him. "The fight was because you helped me."

"Let it go, lady."

He grabbed the hat, slapped it on the back of his head, and grimaced. The horse whinnied. The man swayed, but managed to steady himself before staggering to the animal. "Easy, boy…it's all right."

Maggie grabbed her purse and followed. "Did they hurt your horse?"

"G.W. is fine. Go away."

His harsh words stung, but she didn't give up. "The horse may be fine, but you're not. We should get some help—"

Maggie stopped talking as he untied his horse and led it inside the trailer. She leaned against the cool metal surface, tucking a strand of hair behind one ear. The smell of stale hay teased her nose.

Poor baby, the stallion must have been so frightened. Inside, the cowboy's muted cadence soothed the skittish horse. Soothed her, too. Gradually his words faded away. She pressed an ear to the trailer. Nothing.

Was he okay? Had Greeley's men hurt him so bad he'd passed out?

"Damn you, Kyle," she whispered. "Haven't you done enough?"

"You still here?"

Maggie whirled around to find him standing behind her, so close the brim of his Stetson brushed against her hair. His height blocked the overhead glow from the parking-lot lights, casting his face into shadow. His presence overpowered her, but somehow made her feel safe, too.

Safe? Where in the world had that come from?

"The medical clinic is down the street," she said. "You should have someone take a look at your injuries."

He took a swig from a bottle, grimaced and spat bloody water on the ground. Then he splashed a palm full of water over his face and wiped it away with his shirt sleeve. "Why?"

Maggie planted her hands on her hips. "Look, you need to—"

"I don't *need* to do any…"

The cowboy swayed again. She laid a hand against his chest to stop him from crashing into her. "I can't leave until I know you're okay."

His gaze dropped to her hand, then returned to her face. "We're fine."

His whispered words belied the uneven beat of his heart beneath her fingertips. She jerked her hand away. "Your lip's stopped bleeding, but one eye is swollen shut, and you've got a nasty bruise at your temple."

"What? You wanna play doctor?"

His deep whisper sent a flush of heat fanning over Maggie's cheeks. She swallowed hard against the lump lodged in her throat. "I'll play operator and dial 9-1-1."

"No thanks." He moved past her, shuffling toward the truck cab.

She followed. "I don't think you should drive. You could pass out and kill yourself and your horse. Never mind what you might do to someone else."

He tugged on the door, cursing when it wouldn't open. Finally he got it free and crawled into the cab. "Been in enough fights—not hurt bad—not going far, anyway."

Maggie put her hand on the door before he could close it. She stepped up on the truck's running board, and watched him aim for the ignition.

He missed twice before he paused to squint at the keys. "Was planning to look for…a place to sleep."

The low tone of his voice, mixed with a hint of southern twang, grabbed at her in a place she thought long dead. "This is my fault. Please let me help."

He shook his head then his eyes rolled closed, his hands fell to his lap and he slumped against the seat.

"Are you—hello?"

Silence.

Maggie hesitated then gently removed his hat to get a closer look at his face. She braced one hand on his thigh to keep from falling into his lap. Soft denim and powerful muscles lay beneath her fingertips. Her pale-blue handkerchief sat clutched in his hand, the lace trim out of place next to his large, tanned fingers and the coarse texture of his skin. A deep shudder rumbled through his chest, the warm rush of his breath falling against her cheek. His eyes remained closed.

"I'm going to get help." She'd seen enough injuries on the ranch to know he needed medical attention. "I'll be back."

"Don't." She jumped when his fingers tangled with hers. He held tight for a moment then his grip loosened. "I'll…be fine. Please don't…"

The quiet desperation in his voice struck at the deepest part of her heart. Why was he so against letting someone help him?

"Girly, what in hell's bells are you doing?"

Maggie gasped and pulled her hand free. She swung around and looked into a pair of startling blue eyes framed by a shock of white hair. "Willie! You scared me half to death. What are you doing here?"

"Your grandmother took my ride. I saw your truck in the parking lot, and figured on hitching back with you. Darned surprised to find you getting all frisky in a stranger's pickup."

Willie's sharp gaze peered around Maggie. "And with a drunken cowboy. Hoo-wee!"

"He's not drunk." Maggie stepped from the cab. "There was a fight. I've been trying to convince him to let me get help, but he keeps refusing."

"Yep, right up to when he passed out." Willie shoved his hands in his pockets. "You sure he ain't tanked tight?"

Maggie frowned. "I'm sure. Can you take a look at him?"

The old man, more a member of the family than an employee, stared at her for a long moment.

"Please?"

Willie sighed, then nodded and Maggie stepped out of his way. He gently poked and prodded the unconscious man with a sure touch. Finally, he turned, thumbing up the brim of his hat.

"Well, he ain't dead."

"I know that. Should we take him to the clinic?"

"He's got a lot of bruises and took a good clock to his left eye. He's gonna be hurtin' in the morning." Willie stepped away. "But nothing's broken from what I can tell, and his ribs appear okay. His pupils look fine, too, but that don't explain why he's out cold."

"Exhaustion?" Maggie offered. "He said he needed sleep. He's not from around here and doesn't have a place to stay."

"Oh, boy, I know where this is going."

"Willie—"

"Don't 'Willie' me. I've known you all your life, and if it's one thing you can't resist, it's a hard-luck case." He pointed his finger at her. "Don't matter if it's a four-legged or two-legged creature, you've given away more hot meals and places to sleep than anyone I know."

"Yeah, and then they take off for greener pastures. Look, I'm not out to rescue anyone, but we can't leave him here."

Willie crossed his arms, pulling his starched shirt across his bony shoulders. Age stooped his once-tall frame, but he could still look her in the eye. "There's something more going on here."

Maggie sighed. It took a few minutes to fill him in on losing Spence and Charlie, as well as Kyle's sleazy behavior—until this stranger stepped in.

Willie's features hardened as she spoke. He looked at the cowboy again. "So, they paid him back?"

"Yeah. The least I can do is give him a place to sleep and

a decent breakfast in the morning. And I'm not going to get the sheriff involved over something as trivial as Greeley jerking me around."

"What about this guy getting the crap kicked out of him?"

Maggie dropped her hands to her sides, the cowboy's Stetson banging against her leg. "He was adamant. He doesn't want help from the sheriff or anyone else."

Willie grunted. "You check the trailer. I'll move him to the far side of the truck."

Maggie protested, but he cut her off with a wave of his hand. "I ain't gonna let you drive him to the ranch alone. And it's no good if he wakes up and finds a stranger behind the wheel. So it's the three of us."

"Fine," Maggie handed over the cowboy's keys. "My truck can sit here overnight. I'll pick it up tomorrow."

She checked the trailer then climbed into the cab. The cowboy leaned against the door, his face toward the glass. Willie joined them, forcing her to scoot into the middle, pressing her body into the unconscious man from shoulder to knee. His heat radiated through her dress to dance along her skin. The warm night air jumped up another degree as she watched his chest rise and fall in a steady rhythm.

"Margaret Anne, I hope you know what you're doing," she muttered, dropping his hat into his lap.

Willie pulled out of the parking lot and headed for home as fireworks lit the night sky. A half hour later, they turned off to the ranch. Despite his breathing, the cowboy hadn't uttered a sound. If he didn't wake soon, she'd place a call to Doc Cody.

The headlights gleamed over the bunkhouse and barn as they pulled into the drive, and Willie jolted the truck to a stop. "Sorry 'bout that, the brakes on this thing seem to be as old as me." He opened the driver's door and stepped out. "You stay here with sleeping beauty. I'll get the barn doors."

* * *

A gentle rocking caused Landon's head to loll back and forth. He became aware of soft, feminine curves pressed against him and realized for the first time, in a long time, he wasn't alone.

This was a dream. It had to be.

Unlike the nightmares of the past, he welcomed the heat against his body. Desire to nestle closer stirred deep. He was desperate for her scent, her touch. Desperate to believe this was real. He wanted her next to him, on top of him.

Then the warmth and curves moved away and a hard bounce caused his head to snap backwards. A ricochet of piercing light sparked inside his brain near one eye, and then spread to fill his entire body. He tried to move away from the pain, but his legs protested.

Was he sitting up?

He shifted again and pain exploded in his chest. A groan threatened to erupt, consuming every inch of air in his lungs as he forced himself to focus.

Did he hear voices? The sound of a truck door closing? His truck?

The familiar stale odors from the trailer filled his nose and he tried to slow the merry-go-round spinning inside his head.

Think, dammit! What's the last thing you remember?

The sweet scent of fresh linen. No, that didn't make sense. He hadn't slept in a real bed in over a week. But the fragrance managed to make its way through the smells of his truck.

He curled one hand into a fist, crushing cool cotton against his palm. The same whiff of clean sheets, fresh from drying in the hot sun and a cool breeze, washed over his face as the gentle touch of a woman's hand covered his.

Her curves were back, but it wasn't enough. He wanted to feel her against him. This time his body obeyed his silent command, and his hand found a delicate shoulder.

He pulled her toward him, need rushing through him as

he breathed in her cry of surprise. He drew her closer, swiping his tongue over his dry lips before he covered her mouth. Breath rushed inward between supple lips, and his tongue followed.

He didn't care if he was hallucinating. It was too perfect to stop—and he concentrated on his first kiss in four long years.

A minty flavor greeted him as he explored her mouth. He traced the edge of her teeth with his tongue then slipped out past her lips to dart at the corners of her mouth, sweet like a summertime rain. His hand stole across her upper back, sliding across cool, soft fabric until silky hair tangled with his fingers. He angled her across his chest. Her lips moved against his, and a small stab of pain made him groan. She retreated and this time he let her go.

Consciousness pulled at him, and Landon forced his eyes to open.

One obeyed, the other managed only a slit. His hair fell forward, partially blocking his view of feminine fingers lying over his fist. Clutched inside was a lacy handkerchief. Looking up, he focused on the outline of a woman. For a long moment, a pair of wet lips held his attention. Those lips trembled then the tip of her tongue stole out across her bottom lip.

"Oh…are you okay?"

Despite the shakiness of her words, Landon recognized the voice. Soft, sexy and sweet. The same voice that had suckerpunched him the first time she'd offered a breathless token of gratitude. The lady at the fairgrounds. The same lady who'd interrupted him getting his ass kicked and then refused to go away.

Was it a dream? Had he really kissed her?

Landon ignored her question and the pain shooting through his body. "What are—where am I?" He straightened, tunneling his fingers through his hair.

They sat in his parked, idling truck. He peered into the darkness. Thanks to the glow of a porch light, he could make out the outline of a house.

"My place."

He swung around to face her, and the throbbing intensified. Landon cradled his forehead in his hand. "What the hell am I doing here?"

"You needed a place to sleep."

"Lady, are you crazy? You don't know me."

She withdrew to the steering wheel, her face now hidden in the shadows. "Was I supposed to leave you in the parking lot for the sheriff? I guarantee I can provide a more comfortable bed than the local jail."

The image of a barren room with bars flashed before his eyes. It was quickly pushed aside by another image, springing fully formed in his head before he could stop it.

The two of them, in a bed this time, tangled in crisp, clean sheets. Him flat on his back, her hands spread across his shoulders as he cradled her hips. She leaned forward and her curtain of blond hair hid them from the outside—

Landon squeezed his eyes closed to erase the fantasy. Another sharp ache pounded in his head—as demanding as the one pressed against his fly.

"I know I keep asking, but are you—"

"I'm fine." It was a lie, but he sure as hell wasn't going to tell her what was in his mind.

The truck started to move. Landon opened his eyes, and watched her back toward a large barn that loomed out of the darkness.

She slowed to a stop. "Willie's opening the barn doors—"

"Who's Willie?"

"He works here for—"

"I'll help him."

Landon tugged on the door handle and nearly fell out the cab. He grabbed his hat before it hit the ground and slammed the door closed.

The last thing he needed was this angel of mercy asking him

again if he was okay. He wasn't. Wasn't close to being okay after the vision he had of the two of them together.

Where in the hell had that come from?

He'd had plenty of chances to be with a woman since his release. Every town he'd worked in had bars and honky-tonks filled with ladies who didn't care where you came from or where you were going. Women who wanted the attention they weren't getting at home. He'd never been attracted to any of them. Hell, long before his conviction he'd lost any desire to be physically close to the opposite sex.

Amazing what deception could do to a man.

Burying the memory, Landon reached for the barn doors. He shoved, and they opened easily, thanks to the elderly cowboy on the other side. Had this old timer seen what'd happened in the truck? Did he care?

The man offered a curt nod. "Nice to see you on your feet."

Landon nodded in return. "Thanks. You must be Willie."

They moved aside when the trailer crossed the threshold.

G.W. Damn!

He'd started for the barn's interior when another wave of dizziness hit him. Pressing a hand to his forehead, he fought off the unsteadiness and noticed the square piece of blue cloth in his grasp. A deep breath pulled in the smell of fresh linen and a hint of something spicy. It made him feel…peaceful.

He shoved the handkerchief into his jeans, next to the locket, and entered the barn at the same time as his lady rescuer. She flicked a switch and a circle of light sprang to life overhead. The occupants responded with low neighs.

"Hush, now," she said, then turned to him. "Okay, let's get your horse out of this trailer."

Landon watched the woman, still not understanding how he'd ended up with her and this antique cowboy in the first place. He pinched the bridge of his nose, willing away the pain behind his eyes. "Ah, I'm a bit confused—"

"Not surprising considering the blow you've taken to the ol' noggin," Willie said with a hint of mockery. "You look like you've been rode hard and put up wet."

"You told me no sheriff," the woman said, opening the trailer's gate. "But someone had to look you over, and both you and your horse needed a place to sleep. Willie took care of the first, and the second will be done as soon as we get this animal into a clean stall."

Landon dropped his hand and watched as she lowered the ramp to the floor. She put a foot on the edge, but Willie stopped her.

"Some cowboys think of their horses like they do their women." He pulled the lady a few steps back. "Don't want nobody else touching 'em. The first couple of stalls are empty. Take your pick."

Landon stared hard at the old man then nodded and walked inside the trailer. He ran his hand along G.W.'s coat and dropped his head to rest against his warm mane. He drew in the familiar comfort of his friend before backing him out of the trailer and into a stall.

Grabbing his duffel bags and ice chest, he dropped his stuff on a low bench outside the stall. Another bout of dizziness hit him, but he pushed it away.

"She does this a lot."

Landon looked up, surprised to see it was only him and Willie in the barn.

"Can't resist helping someone who's downtrodden," Willie continued. "Been that way since she was a little bit. Doesn't matter if it's a rangy dog or a broke-down cowboy, she's always there to offer a hot meal and a warm bed."

Landon didn't know which the old man considered him to be. "Is that so?"

"She doesn't expect anything in return and that's usually what she gets, but I've been here since God was a boy, and

part of my job is looking out for my boss. I don't want her
hurt."

Wait a minute.

Landon blinked. Did he say *boss?*

Chapter Three

"Yeah, you heard me right. She's the one in charge around here. We haven't been properly introduced. Willie Perkins." He stuck out his hand.

Landon took it, not surprised at the strong grip. "Landon Cartwright."

"At least you know who ya are. Come on, I'll fix ya up in the bunk—"

"No, thanks. I'll stay here."

Willie's bushy white brows arched high. "In the barn?"

Landon pulled his hand free. "Yeah, I've slept in worse places. Believe it or not, I've been in fights before, too."

"Now, why don't that surprise me? We got enough trouble around here, you hear?"

"Look, old man. I didn't ask for her help. Or yours. And trouble is the last thing I'm looking for."

Willie stared back at him for a long moment, then nodded. "Fair enough. I'll park your truck by the house. You get the doors."

He didn't wait for a reply. Minutes later, Willie walked by and tossed him the keys before disappearing into the bunkhouse. Pocketing them, Landon closed one barn door, then stopped. His eyes drifted across the yard to the light spilling from a window in the main house.

Who was this lady? Did she own this spread? Alone?

Willie hadn't mentioned a husband, and she seemed pretty upset with Greeley back at the carnival. He couldn't remember if she wore a wedding ring, not that a piece of jewelry kept someone faithful.

And this ranch.

Other than the outlines of a few buildings, including a one-story house with a wraparound porch, he couldn't see much in the darkness. The quiet surprised him. The barn sounded as if it was full of horses, but except for Willie, there weren't any other cowboys in sight, and only one other pickup besides his own.

Unusual for a Saturday night and a holiday...

Stop thinking so much. Landon shut the other barn door. *You've got more important things to worry about.*

His body was wracked with sharp twinges of pain as he moved toward the stalls. After closer inspection of G.W.'s leg, he was happy to see the swelling under control.

"Wish I had some liniment to help you out, boy." He kept his voice soft as he rewrapped the leg with firm pressure. "We'll have to rely on good ol' cold and hot therapy until I can get more cash."

G.W. responded with a flick of his ears. A twinge of guilt twisted through Landon as he watched his horse feed. After a week of foraging on the side of the road, it was clear the palomino was enjoying the fresh hay and water.

Landon left the stall and walked to the bench. A low groan escaped as he pulled off his boots. It took a minute for another wave of dizziness to pass before he emptied his pockets into the duffel bag. He kept the tarnished silver locket. It took all his strength not to open it and look inside.

Rubbing his fingers over the inlaid scrollwork, he stared at it for a long moment then shoved it back into his jeans. Not now. He couldn't deal with any more pain tonight.

What was left of his shirt hung free and he undid the few remaining buttons before releasing the top button of his jeans. His shoulders and arms ached as he reached around to rub the scar tissue on his lower back. He could get the crap kicked out of him and the injury didn't flare up. Then something as simple as changing a tire and—

Injury. Yeah, right.

Injury implied healing. Not this. This he would carry for the rest of his life. He peeled the shirt off his shoulders. A low creaking caused him to spin around.

"I'm sorry. I didn't mean to startle you." She walked from the shadows, her arms filled with blankets, a pillow and a glass of water. "Willie called me from the bunkhouse and said you'd be staying…"

A rush of heat spread across Landon's skin when her gaze trailed from his face, past his open shirt to his feet, then back again. Brightness shone in her emerald eyes. The pink on her cheeks matched her full lips and the memory of their imaginary kiss came rushing back.

He didn't know if she was married or not, but the intensity of her stare was enough to start the pressure building behind his fly for the second time tonight.

"I guess I should've knocked first."

Landon forced himself to relax. He tugged his shirt back onto his shoulders, thankful he still wore his hat. "It's your barn."

She held out the bedding in her arms and frowned. "Why sleep out here?"

"I already told your cowboy. The place is clean and the hay's fresh. Better than where I've slept the last few days." Landon's heart pounded as he took the blankets, warm from her body. The now-familiar scent of fresh linen drifted around him. "Besides, most cowboys don't welcome sharing a bunk-house with an outsider. And I'm sure your husband isn't too crazy about you bringing home a total stranger."

He placed the items on the bench then turned to find her holding out the glass in one hand, two pills in the other and a faint blush on her cheeks.

"You might be right about the cowboys, but not the husband. I don't have one." She pushed the glass and pills at him. "Here, you must have one heck of a headache."

No husband.

He ignored the jolt the news gave him, looked at the pills instead. He hesitated, hating how three years in prison had colored his view of people. He doubted the pills were anything other than pain medication. How could he refuse? She'd done more for him, a total stranger, than anyone else since he'd gotten out.

"You said your ranch hand checked me out?" He took the glass. "How did he do that exactly?"

"Willie served in the Korean War as a medic." She dropped the medicine into his hand. "He has a bit of medical school under his belt, too. He's helped a lot of people around here over the years."

Landon nodded before he tipped his head back and pre-tended to take the pills. Instead, he slipped them into his pocket and washed the dryness from his mouth with the cool water.

"So, you all set?" She moved past him toward the horse stalls. "Got enough pillows, blankets…liniment?"

"Excuse me?"

"You told me those men didn't hurt your horse." She stood at G.W.'s stall and grabbed the top edge of the split door. "But I saw him favoring his forelimb when you brought him out of the trailer."

He joined her, but stayed at arm's length. "They didn't hurt him. His injury happened about a week ago. Tonight's excitement didn't help."

She took the glass from his outstretched hand. "Neither did riding in your trailer."

G.W. shook his head and offered a nicker in response. She grinned and held her hand flat for the horse's inspection before laying her palm on his nose and gently rubbing.

Another stabbing pain pierced Landon's chest. This one didn't hurt like the others. Laced with an edge of something carnal, it curled inside his gut.

He put more space between them and crossed his arms over his chest. The sawdust covering the concrete floor was cool against his feet. "He's okay. I've got it under control."

"I've got Dermcusal, but it might be too late." She offered the horse a final pat before moving away. "Warming liniments might help. There's a refrigerator and warmer in the tack room."

"Lady, what are you—"

"Wait right here." She disappeared through a door in the corner of the barn. He could hear the jingling of keys, then she returned with a jumble of small boxes and tubes that she handed to him. "Here, these should help. If you want, we can call Kali Watson in the morning. She's the local vet, well, the practice is her and her husband, but he's gone at the moment—"

"No."

Landon's reply was stronger than he intended, evident by how she skittered backwards. He looked at the medicine he'd been hoping for a moment ago. Medicine he couldn't afford.

"Ah, no thanks." His voice was softer this time. "I can care for him."

"How? You said you didn't have anywhere to go tonight."

"I did? When?"

"Back at the fairgrounds when we debated whether you were fit to drive." She took another step toward the side door. "That's how you ended up here."

Geez, he needed to clear the fog swirling in his head. What else had he said?

He again looked at the tubes of ointment and swallowed hard. "I appreciate this, but I'm passing through. I can't...I don't have the money to pay you."

She waved off his words. "Don't worry about it."

Pride filled him. He'd always earned everything he'd gotten in life. Long before his time in jail, charity wasn't something he'd ever taken lightly. "And the hay—G.W. can eat like there's no tomorrow. Your hospitality—"

"Consider it a proper thank you for what you did for me tonight." She reached behind her and opened the door. "You know, with all that's happened you never did tell me your name."

"Cartwright." The word was out of his mouth before he thought about it. "Landon Cartwright."

"Well, Landon Cartwright, my name's Maggie Stevens. Welcome to the Crescent Moon. You're invited to breakfast come morning if you're still here."

She hurried through the door, closing it firmly behind her. Landon remained rooted to the spot and stared after her before he dumped the meds on the bench.

Had he heard right?

He pulled the help-wanted ad from his jeans.

Yep, Crescent Moon.

Bam, bam, bam.

Maggie allowed one eye to open wide enough to look at the clock on her nightstand. A low groan escaped her lips. Despite the morning light filling her bedroom, it wasn't quite six o'clock. Unlike most nights when she'd fall into bed already half asleep, it'd taken hours before she'd stopped reliving the events of last night. For a day that started so simply, it certainly ended with a bang.

More like an explosion.

She pictured the tall, handsome stranger sleeping in her barn and relived his soul-stirring, stomach-dropping kiss. The memory made Maggie's insides plunge all the way to her toes.

The same as they did last night when Landon had grabbed her and pulled her close in his truck. She had seen his head snap back against the seat rest when Willie had hit the brakes. Her first instinct had been to make sure he was okay. His first instinct, evidently, had been to cover her mouth with his. She'd been so surprised by his actions and her response that it had taken a groan from him to make her pull away.

Racy was always telling her she needed a little excitement in her life. Nothing like breaking up a fight and bringing home a not-so-conscious sexy stranger to liven things up.

A stranger who cared very much for his horse.

Intuition told her the cowboy and G.W. were best friends, despite the sad conditions of both his truck and trailer. Maybe it was because he'd wanted to stay in the barn. Or the relief in his eyes when he'd first seen the medicine. A relief quickly hidden behind a mask of pride.

Bam, bam, bam.

Maggie groaned again and crawled from her bed. She crossed to one of the windows facing the barn. It had to be Hank. No matter how many times she'd told him it was okay to start the workday a little later on Sundays, he was always up at dawn. Thanks to ranch hands disappearing and the list of chores growing daily, she was up with the sun most days, too. Hank had agreed to do something away from the house until everyone else was up and moving. But not this morning. No, it sounded as if he was right beneath her window.

White eyelet curtains ruffled in the cool morning breeze, obscuring her view. She pulled them to the side and squinted at the cloudless blue sky and the promise of another hot summer day. She scanned the swimming hole in the backyard and the empty foreman's cabin until her eyes came to rest on the tall figure wielding a hammer at the main corral.

That wasn't Hank.

There was no way anyone could confuse her ranch hand, a shorter, solid, fatherly type, with the man outside her window. A lean, muscular body poured into a black T-shirt and matching jeans, stood tall in the morning light. His long hair was tied at the base of his neck under a black Stetson.

"Landon Cartwright," Maggie whispered against the windowpane.

He dug into a pocket before dropping to a crouch. Her next breath came out in a low hum as the denim covering his backside pulled taut. His shirt did the same over muscular arms and shoulders as he lifted a wooden slat. He braced it with his knee, and then—*bam, bam, bam*—three blows of the hammer sank three nails to secure the board in place.

Okay, that was impressive.

He rose and circled the corral, stopping to test each section, making quick work of an important job she hadn't had time to tackle in the last month.

Thanks to the work she'd done with a horse for Destiny's mayor and the fact that his wife was a cousin of Tucker Hargrove, she'd won first crack at taming a horse purchased by the A-list movie star for his talented but spoiled daughter. Black Jack, a wild mustang who fit his name perfectly, was due to arrive the day after next.

Landon stopped and turned, his gaze narrowing on her window.

Maggie dropped the curtain and scooted to the side, bracing herself against the flowery wallpaper. Her heart raced.

"He's a man doing ordinary chores," she chided, ignoring the butterflies in her stomach. "Get over it."

She wished it were that easy. His dark eyes and calloused yet gentle touch had haunted her deep into the night. Willie was right. She'd brought home another stray. Without a second thought to the pile of bills on her desk, she'd handed over medicine she should've kept for her own horses.

But she couldn't stop herself.

The palomino was a beauty, with its golden coat, dark eyes, and white mane and tail. Its owner was a cowboy who'd stepped in when most would've minded their own business, and got the crap kicked out of him for his troubles.

A cowboy who was now finishing one of the many chores at her ranch.

A cowboy who'd kissed her, but likely wouldn't even remember.

It was for the best.

With all last night's excitement, she hadn't given a second thought to what the loss of her ranch hands would mean until long after she'd crawled into bed. Once again, she toyed with the idea of talking to this stranger about the job. Lord knows she needed the help, but should she take the first cowboy that sashayed down the road?

The air remained silent. Maggie glanced past the edge of the curtain in time to see his knees hit the ground as he grabbed on to the side of the corral.

She raced from her bedroom, out the back door and across the cool, green grass and the dusty, dirt-packed drive. When she reached him, he was back on his feet, but bent at the waist.

"Are you all right?"

He took his time rising to his full height. One hand rubbed his stomach, pulling the fabric of his shirt tight across his chest. The other hung at his side, the hammer clenched in his fist. His dark eyes roamed over her, from her bed-head hair to her naked toes.

"Is that Clint Eastwood?"

Maggie followed his pointed gaze, and let loose a low groan, her face and neck growing hot. Her pajamas consisted of a tank top, emblazed with a head shot of the legendary actor, and matching loose cotton pants, covered with horseshoes and saddles, that hung low on her waist.

"They were a gift." She fidgeted. "Are you sure you're okay?"

He tugged his Stetson lower. "Tired. I was up most of the night with G.W."

"How is he?"

"Fine."

Maggie waited for him to go into detail, but the firm press of his lips told her he was finished.

"But you're not."

He stared at her for a long moment. Maggie returned his gaze. With his dark skin and hat pulled low, it was hard to see the varying shades of the shiner around his eye, but at least he was able to open it. Her toes curled into the dirt under his steady gaze.

"I'm fine, too," he said at last.

"Better than fine the way you wielded that hammer."

"I didn't know I had an audience."

A flush of heat stained Maggie's cheeks. "Things are pretty quiet around here on Sunday mornings."

"Well, after waking to find a shotgun in my face—"

"What?"

"I think I surprised one of your ranch hands." He shoved a hand into the front pocket of his jeans. "I told him I had permission to camp in the barn. I guess he believed me because he let me help muck the stalls and feed the horses. He then saddled up and left."

Maggie heaved a sigh. "Hank Jarvis. He's my other hand. Did he say anything else?"

Landon cleared his throat. "He mumbled something about a soft-hearted do-gooder."

"That would be me." Maggie crossed her arms, conscious she wasn't wearing a bra. "So, you want to explain why you're fixing my corral?"

"I figured since I was awake I'd do something to thank you for the meds, putting me up last night…everything."

"Last night was my way of thanking you for helping me with that pain-in-the-ass Greeley," Maggie countered, "and getting beat up for your efforts."

"I told you—"

"Yeah, you told me." Maggie propped her hands on her hips. "Don't let the fact I'm a natural blonde fool you. I'm not as dumb as I look. Not anymore, and—"

"Margaret Anne Stevens! What in the blazes are you doing out here half-naked? And talking with a stranger, no less!"

Maggie jumped and spun around. Her grandmother, five feet of wiry enthusiasm and pure white curls, stood on the back porch. "Nana B., you scared me!" Then she sighed, and turned back to Landon. "My grandmother. You might as well come meet her before she goes for her shotgun, too."

His mouth twitched at one corner.

Maggie started across the yard, a hot prickle dancing across her skin. As much as she wanted to blame it on the July sun, she wondered if it was Landon's heated gaze on her back.

And her backside.

"I'm not half-naked and this isn't a stranger…well, not really." Maggie pushed her hair from her eyes as she reached the porch. Turning, she found he'd stayed at the foot of the stairs. "This is Landon and he—ah, he and his horse needed a place to crash last night. Landon Cartwright, my grandmother, Beatrice Travers."

"Ma'am." He hooked one finger on the brim of his Stetson and nodded.

"Call me Nana B., everyone does." Her grandmother shot Maggie a quick look then continued. "So, you're the noisemaker. You look right at home with a hammer. We're lookin'—"

"Nana B.!" Horror filled Maggie at her grandmother's words. "Mr. Cartwright isn't looking for work."

"I'm passing through, ma'am."

Nana B.'s back stiffened, then a bright smile danced over her aged features. "Not without washing up and some breakfast." She headed back inside. "I'll get started on the food, you two get wet."

Get wet.

The two little words sent Maggie's heart racing again. Last night's fantasy of a midnight skinny-dip, present company included, flashed inside her head. Mortified, she bit her bottom lip, glancing toward Landon. "Ah, there's a half bath inside if you want it."

His gaze dropped to her lips. Something hot and powerful flashed in his dark eyes. Her nipples tightened against the soft cotton of her tank top. His eyes flickered to her breasts for a moment before looking away.

A muscle ticked in his jaw as he focused on the horizon. "I should be heading out."

A voice deep inside, frantic and desperate, cried out for him to stay.

Good Lord, where'd that come from?

"N-not without breakfast. My grandmother would skin me alive if I let you leave before tasting her blue-ribbon muffins." She backed up until her butt hit the door. She pulled it open and stepped inside. "Besides, your horse is going to need—"

"I know what G.W. needs."

The screen door banged closed between them at his abrupt words. Maggie didn't know him from a hole in the wall. Her gut told her he was a good man, but hell, she'd been wrong before. Her body's reaction was a poor barometer. She had her family and ranch to protect. Besides, it was clear he wanted to leave.

"Fine...do what you want."

She forced herself not to look back as she made a beeline for the bathroom. The phone on the hall table rang. She grabbed the extension before it stopped. "Crescent Moon."

"Mama?"

Joy flooded Maggie at the sound of her daughter's voice. "Hey, sweetie."

"Are you okay? Did I wake you?"

"I'm fine, honey, and no, you didn't wake me." *A tall, sexy-as-sin cowboy who's no doubt packing his truck as we speak, did.* "Why are you calling so early?"

A long pause filled the air. "I wanted to check on things."

Oh, Anna. Maggie leaned again the wall and pressed a hand to her forehead. *Eight years old is too young to be such a worrier.* "Everything is fine here."

"No accidents while we were at the carnival?"

"You know Hank stayed at the ranch while we were in town." Maggie straightened and forced a smile into her words. "Did you and Julie have a good time last night?"

She listened to her daughter's excited chatter for a few more minutes before ending the call. After lingering under the spray of the shower, she grabbed her robe and headed to her bedroom. Once inside, she paused at the door. Despite the nearness of her room to the kitchen, she didn't hear a word of conversation.

Not her grandmother's lilting pitch, which still carried a hint of her Irish heritage, or Willie's gravel-filled murmur that reminded her of aged leather. And certainly not the low, smoky tone of her rescuer-cowboy.

Girl, you've got more important things to worry about than a cowboy and his lame horse. She closed the door and moved to her dresser. *Like the financial standing of your ranch.*

Financial leaning was a better way to put it.

After pulling on her boots, she used the hair dryer to blast her shoulder-length hair then pulled it into a ponytail as columns of figures from her so-called budget flashed through her mind. An upcoming vet payment to the Watson Clinic loomed, and her credit line at the feed store was near its limit. Not to mention the final balloon payment on the loan she'd had to get to buy her ex out of the Crescent Moon.

Balloon payment! What a stupid term for a financial dealing. Made it sound like something connected with a birthday party instead of a way for her to lose everything.

Lose everything? Over my dead body.

Maggie marched into the kitchen, drawn by the aroma of her grandmother's cooking. Weaving her leather belt through the loops on her jeans, she walked right into a heated wall of muscles.

Chapter Four

"Watch out!" Landon cried out. "Hot coffee!"

"Oh!" Maggie grabbed on to the front of his shirt.

With one arm clamped around her waist, he swung her in a neat circle. He held a mug away from them, managing not to spill a drop. "You're in a bit of a hurry, aren't you?"

She looked up. Despite the height difference—he easily carried six or more inches on her—she noticed how perfectly they fit together. Without his hat and his dark hair pulled back from his face, the sharp angles of his nose and cheekbones were more prominent.

Maggie's stomach zoomed for another roller-coaster ride. She forced herself to look away, her eyes centering on his chest. Her blood ran cold.

She pushed, and he released her. "Where did you get that shirt?"

"I gave it to him." Nana B. set two plates of food on the table.

"No sense waiting on Willie. The old coot probably can't pull himself away from the mirror. You two eat."

Landon grabbed an empty chair, but remained standing. Maggie stared at him until she realized he was waiting on her. She fumbled with her belt, getting it tight against her stomach, before she pulled out her chair and sat.

He followed. "It was either this shirt or nothing. All of my stuff is wet."

"What?"

"I started his laundry." Nana B. placed another plate of food on the table as Willie entered the kitchen. "It's about time, Handsome."

Maggie's eyes shifted from Willie's cheeks, marked by embarrassment, to her grandmother. "You did what?"

Landon put his napkin on his lap. "After washing up I walked out of the bathroom and found your grandmother waiting with a steaming mug of coffee in one hand and this shirt in the other."

"One whiff of the duffel bag he'd brought in told me he needed his skivvies cleaned, and cleaned good," Nana B. said. "So, I dumped it all in the washer. Then I demanded his T-shirt, too."

"I've been on the road the last week and haven't—she said I wasn't going to eat until I changed." Landon offered a careless shrug. "After catching the scent of eggs and bacon, I did what I was told."

"Which is usually best when dealing with my grandmother," Maggie said, staring at the older woman.

"Makes sense to help him out." Nana B. offered an arched brow in response as she joined them. "If he's gonna work here."

"I told you he's not—"

"I told you I'm not—"

Landon's words collided with Maggie's, and they both stopped short.

"Mr. Cartwright fixed the corral in less than an hour," Nana B. said while buttering her toast. "Isn't that amazing? Maggie's been after Spence to get it done for a week now. Speaking of that youngster, think we might see him and his sidekick crawl outta the bunkhouse anytime soon?"

Maggie set her coffee mug on the table. "Ah, Nana, I should've told you before you started cooking. Spence and Charlie quit last night. They're working for Greeley now."

"They're what?" Nana B. cried out, her knife clanging against her plate. "Those no-good, snot-nose saplings! What are we going to—"

Maggie cut her off. "Let's talk about it after breakfast, okay?"

Silence filled the sunny country kitchen. The only sound came from Willie, who seemed determined to finish his breakfast in record time.

Nana B. frowned, then replaced it with another bright smile. "Whatever you say, dearie. Mr. Cartwright can be on his way as soon as I'm done fluffin' and foldin'."

"Ah, ma'am, I can handle my own laundry—"

"Don't you never mind." Nana B. cut Landon's protest off with a wink. "Considering the quick work you did this morning, we owe you a debt of thanks. Now eat before it gets cold."

Landon glanced between Maggie and her grandmother before he turned to his food and dug in.

Maggie did the same, not completely trusting her grandmother's scheming mind. Not that she could do anything about it now. If the woman thought corralling Landon was a way to help, she'd try to do it.

Not that Maggie wasn't trying to hire more cowboys, but after finding Kyle sweet-talking Spence and Charlie, she'd bet his long reach extended to the whole county, keeping anyone from answering her ads.

Except for his former employee who sat at her kitchen table.

"So, cowboy, where you from?"

Willie's question broke the silence. Maggie gave Landon an expectant look.

"No place special," he said. "I finished a drive for the Red River Ranch in Blakeslee, Colorado. I've never been to this part of the country before, so I decided to head this way."

"How long were you at Red River?" Nana B. asked.

Landon paused for a long moment. Maggie got the feeling if it was anyone else asking, he'd tell 'em to mind their own business. "About a month. Before that the Double Deuce outside of Las Vegas, and the Circle S near Tucson."

"You move around a lot." The words were out of Maggie's mouth before she could pull them back.

His lips pressed into a hard line before he spoke. "There's a lot of country to see."

He's a drifter. Maggie put the thought firmly at the front of her brain as she resumed eating.

Landon forced his attention away from Maggie's mesmerizing green eyes and back to his plate. Her folded ad burned in the back pocket of his jeans.

Should he stay or should he go?

The question swirled inside his head, much as it'd done all night. After getting a good look at the Crescent Moon in the daylight, he understood why Maggie and her grandmother were upset about losing two more cowboys. They needed help. A lot of help.

Most of the buildings could do with repairs and fresh paint. He'd found the tools to fix the corral in a shed that looked ready to topple at a strong wind. Here in the kitchen the linoleum flooring curled in places and the appliances were a shade of avocado green that dated them back three decades. He didn't know how many head of cattle or acres of land she had, but he'd tended to almost a dozen horses in the barn this morning.

How was she going to handle it all with her grandmother and two geriatric cowboys?

Two ladies and two old geezers. Too much like family for

him. At one time, family had been a big part of his life. The biggest. Not anymore. And he had no one to blame but himself.

"You got another job lined up?"

Another nosy question from Willie broke into his thoughts. Landon looked up and found all three watching him. He took a sip of strong, black coffee. "On the other side of the Black Hills."

That was a lie. When he'd been forced from his last job, a fellow cowboy had told him about a place, saying they were always looking for help. What he didn't have was enough money to get from Wyoming to South Dakota.

"I guess you'll want to head out soon, seeing as it's a couple days' drive," Maggie said.

His gaze held hers. "Yeah, you're probably right."

She pursed her lips then returned to eating. This time he couldn't look away from the fork sliding between her lips. The memory of his mouth on hers flashed through his mind.

Had they or hadn't they?

He still wasn't sure if the kiss in his truck was real or a fantasy. He raised his gaze, surprised at the quick flash of heat in her eyes. Was she thinking the same thing?

Probably not, he decided when her eyes flickered away and centered on his chest, her lips flattening into a hard line. She'd frowned like that earlier when she'd pushed him away. Good thing, too, or else she would've realized the effect her body had on his.

Another reason to get the hell out of here.

What exactly occurred between the two of them last night was a bit fuzzy, but having her in his arms again this morning made one thing clear. He'd put his hands on her. And not to steady her or keep her from falling. No, he'd held her close, pulled her up hard against him in order to feel the intimate details of her soft curves.

"Bats wingin' around the belfry?"

Landon looked at Willie. "Excuse me?"

"The way you're shaking your head makes me wonder if we should be hearin' a rattling noise or the thrapping of wings."

"Thrapping?"

"Yeah, you know." Willie dropped his fork and knife, tucked his fingers under his armpits, and waved his bent arms. "Thrap, thrap, thrap."

Nana B. frowned at Willie. "Old man, you've taken one too many horseshoes to the head." Then she smiled at Landon. "More food, Mr. Cartwright?"

"No, thank you, ma'am." Her generous helpings had filled his empty stomach. He ignored Willie's question and rose, putting his plate and utensils in the sink. "I wouldn't mind another cup of coffee, though."

"Help yourself." Nana B. pointed to the counter. "The coffee maker runs twenty-four hours a day around here."

He filled his mug with the steaming liquid. He could feel Maggie's gaze on him.

"You need more food, honey?"

Landon turned to lean against the counter just as Maggie's grandmother asked her the question. She snapped her attention back to her plate, a faint blush on her cheeks. "Are you kidding?" she said, jabbing at the remains of her eggs. "There's too much here already."

"Hogwash! You're too skinny, like those girls on that castaway show. Now, finish up."

Willie guffawed behind his coffee mug. Landon did the same, though more quietly. Too skinny? No way.

He'd been right last night about her dress hiding her curves. They were in plain sight today, thanks to a soft, gray T-shirt and faded jeans hugging her in all the right places. A ponytail made her look about eighteen, probably ten years younger than her true age.

"Well, the day's a-wasting." Willie rose, wiping his mouth

with a napkin. He placed his dishes in the sink before grabbing a ragged, straw Stetson from a hook near the door. "I'm gonna meet up with Hank and check the herd. Unless you need me here?"

Willie eyed Landon and Maggie followed his gaze.

"No, we'll be fine," she said. "Oh, my truck. I've got to get into town—"

"I'll take you," he interrupted.

Her green eyes returned to his, and he found himself wishing for his hat.

"I thought you were leaving?" she asked.

He was. So why weren't his feet moving?

Placing his mug on the counter, he shoved his hands into the front pockets of his jeans. "I'll drop you off on my way out."

She didn't reply.

"Margaret Anne, where are your manners?" Nana B. chided. "Say thank you."

"Thank you," she dutifully repeated, looking away as she rose.

Landon nodded, not believing she meant it and wondering why he cared. "I'll finish up my laundry so we can head out."

"I told you not to worry about that." Nana B. dried her hands with a dishrag. "It's gonna be a couple of hours before you can leave anyway."

"A couple hours?"

Maggie walked to the sink and dumped her dishes into the soapy water. "The machine's old. It takes a few cycles to get everything dry."

"Dryer-schmryer. I'll put this beautiful day to good use and hang most of it outside. Nothing like the smell of clean clothes fresh from flapping in the sunshine." Nana B. draped the dish towel over Maggie's shoulder and winked before walking into the mudroom.

Fresh linen.

The memory of that scent invading his dreams caused

Landon to draw in a deep breath. There it was again, mixed among the lingering smells of frying bacon and lemon dish soap. Since he'd held Maggie in his arms, her fresh, unsullied fragrance clung to his clothes, and his fingers itched at the awakened memory of soft skin.

Willie cleared his throat. "I'll be heading out, then."

Maggie nodded. "See you at dinner."

Willie nodded and moved to Landon. "I guess I'll say my goodbyes."

Landon took his outstretched hand. "Much obliged for—well, for last night."

"No need. You helped Miss Maggie with that jackass Gree—" Willie's eyes darted to Maggie's grandmother busy at the washing machine. His voice dropped to a mumble. "—and we helped you."

"Is he as much of a weasel as he pretends to be?" Landon asked, ending the handshake.

"Yes siree."

"No."

Maggie's disagreement had Landon locking gazes with her across the kitchen. Her eyes held for a moment then broke free, and she busied herself clearing the table. He looked back at the elderly cowboy.

"You didn't take a beatin' for no reason," Willie muttered before heading out. The sound of the back door closing echoed through the kitchen.

Landon moved toward the table, keeping his voice soft. "You told Willie about your run-in with Greeley. But not your grandmother?"

Maggie ignored him as she put things away in the refrigerator.

He leaned closer and asked, "She accepts a stranger who spent the night in your barn and ends up at her table the next morning?"

"Not much surprises my grandmother anymore." Maggie closed the fridge door, pausing to push hard against the handle until it clicked shut.

"Why didn't you tell her?"

She spun around, her honey-colored hair whipping over her shoulder. "What happened last night was no big deal."

Landon crossed his arms over his chest, ignoring the need to brush away the few strands caught at the edge of her mouth. "You get manhandled, break up fights and bring home strangers often?"

First surprise, then anger crossed Maggie's features. She advanced on him until they stood toe to toe. "You don't know me. You don't know this ranch. And you sure as hell made it clear you don't want to work here. So why don't you mind your own business?"

She pushed past him and stomped across the kitchen.

He watched her go, a grin playing at the corner of his mouth. Maggie Stevens had a temper, and she was sexy as hell when riled.

No, don't go there. You're halfway out the door.

Still, his gut told him something wasn't right. He didn't know if it was Maggie's refusal to tell her grandmother about last night or the fact she'd brought home a total stranger and treated him like family.

Forget it. You don't know these people from a hole in the wall, and you've got your own problems to deal with like an empty wallet and a lame horse.

Ah, hell.

He started for the back door, grabbing his hat on the way out. Maggie headed across the yard. He followed her into the cool interior of the barn. "Hold on a minute—"

"I don't have time to hold on." Maggie moved from one empty stall to the next, pausing to open each door and push it flat against the wall. "In case you haven't noticed, I've a lot of work to do."

The words were out of his mouth before he could stop them. "Where do I start?"

She paused a moment, then grabbed a pitchfork and walked into the first stall. "You don't."

He followed, pulling her ad from his back pocket. "I thought you were looking for cowboys."

"You thought wrong," she snapped, turning around. Her gaze zoomed to the folded piece of paper in his hands. "Where did you get that?"

"From the general store in town." Landon stepped farther into the stall. "Right before I got jumped."

Pain filled her eyes at his reminder. "It's an old ad."

He fingered the worn, dirtied edges but kept his eyes trained on hers. "You need help around here. Now more than ever."

"No, what I need is to be more efficient." She turned back to a bale of straw, and attacked it. "And to mind *my* own business."

Landon fought the impulse to walk away. He couldn't. He owed her. She was in trouble up to her neck, but she wasn't asking for help. In fact, she'd opened herself up to more trouble by bringing him home when she should've left his sorry ass in the parking lot.

He watched her toss the straw around the stall with her pitchfork, something valiant in the set of her shoulders.

"I'll take the job," he said abruptly.

She stopped and looked at him. "Why?"

A loud whinny from G.W. prevented him from answering as they both rushed to his stall. Landon got there first and found his horse pawing at the fresh hay on the ground.

"Whoa there, boy." He dropped to his knees and put his hands on G.W.'s injured leg.

"What is it? I thought you said he was okay."

Maggie leaned in to look over his shoulder, her curves pressing against his back. Heat stole through his shirt and he bit back a groan.

"Ah, the inflammation hasn't dropped. G.W. hates these pressure bandages."

"Most horses do." She moved to rub the horse's nose and the stallion quieted. "He's beautiful."

Landon refused to think about the loss of her body heat and concentrated on removing the bandage. "Yeah, he's pretty impressive."

"Where'd you get him?"

His hands stilled. Anger flashed hot inside. "He's mine, bought and paid for. I have the papers if you want to see them."

"What? Oh, you thought I—that's crazy."

She wasn't going to question his ownership of the stallion. The men he'd worked for over the past months always had. Then again, she was no man. Maggie was all woman. Soft, sexy and right here in front of him.

Landon looked up and found her stomach at eye level. The snug fit of her jeans over her hips and thighs registered first in his brain, and then throughout his body.

She might be your boss now. You'd better remember that.

He forced his attention back to the horse. G.W. responded with a gentle nicker that Landon took for pleasure at either losing the bandage or the way Maggie continued to stroke him.

"His name, the initials G.W. Do they stand for anything?" she asked.

"Georgia's Wind, after his mother."

"Have you ever thought about putting him out to stud?"

"I did once. The foal didn't make it." He pushed the memory from his head, and stood. "He's the reason."

"Huh?"

"You asked why I want this job. You can see for yourself he's hurting." Landon latched onto the obvious. "I don't want to move him. We've been through a lot together over the— anyway, he needs time to rest and recover."

"So you're looking for something temporary?"

Yeah, the shorter, the better. "Until G.W. is healed."

Her mouth curved into a wistful smile. "The paint in the last stall is mine. Rowdy's my best friend, too. He was born the same month I graduated high school. We've been together for the last twelve years."

Landon understood the pride in her voice. G.W. had been a college graduation present from his folks. They'd hoped he'd forget his dream of the rodeo and return home. Instead, he and G.W. had burned up the calf-roping circuit for three years straight. Until a phone call changed everything.

A familiar sting forced him to blink hard and look away.

"Well, I guess that settles it," Maggie said. "Hey, you all ri— oh!"

Landon's eyes flew open the moment the warmth of Maggie's hands and then her body, landed solidly on his chest. Grabbing her upper arms, he braced his legs to keep them both from tumbling to the ground.

Over Maggie's shoulder, G.W. bobbed his head. Landon realized his buddy was playing an old game. He found himself grinning in response, until his gaze returned to the woman in his arms.

Her eyes, wide with surprise, collided with his. A rush of warm breath caressed the bare skin at the open collar of his shirt. He swiped at his lips, his gaze firmly planted on the enticing mouth before him.

He shouldn't. She was his boss. Despite his wonderings over what had happened last night, this wasn't a good idea. In fact, it was a real wrong idea. Her lips parted and he dipped his head—

"Well, well, what's going on here?"

Landon jerked away from Maggie at the sound of the silky-smooth male voice. Releasing his hold, he immediately tucked her behind him.

"A bit territorial, aren't we, Cartwright?" Kyle Greeley

stood in the center aisle of the barn and grinned. "Well, it seems I'm not the only one who enjoys spending time with Maggie Stevens in deserted barns."

Chapter Five

Kyle's words caused the faded scar at Maggie's hairline to burn as if still fresh.

Six months ago a dinner date ended with Kyle giving her a tour of his new state-of-the-art barn. Minutes later, he'd cornered her, expecting something in return. Her knee barely missed crippling him, and his ring caught her high on the forehead. He claimed it was an accident. Too humiliated, she kept her mouth shut and ended the budding relationship.

Maggie shoved the memory away and moved out from behind Landon. "What are you doing here, Kyle?"

"What the hell is *he* doing here? And wearing a Crescent Moon shirt?"

Landon took a step toward Kyle.

Maggie moved between them. "What do you want?"

Kyle's eyes moved from her face to stare over the top of her head. "Do you mind? We'd like a little privacy."

"What do *you* want, Maggie?" Landon's words whispered hot over her ear.

"Why don't you do something useful," Kyle said. "Like take out the trash."

"With pleasure."

Landon moved from behind her. Maggie's restraining hand shot out and landed on a denim-clad, rock-hard thigh.

Oh, boy, this wasn't good. On so many levels.

She yanked her hand away, tried to ignore the sensations dancing along her arm and looked over her shoulder. Full lips, pressed into a firm line, made the angle of Landon's jaw appear hard as stone. Faint discoloration around his eye and the slight swelling at the corner his mouth reminded her it was Kyle's men who'd jumped him last night. Because of her.

"Landon, why don't you finish here?" Another display of male testosterone was the last thing either of them needed. "I'll take this outside."

His eyes narrowed in a silent threat. "Fine."

Maggie waved toward the barn doors. Greeley turned and headed out. She followed him into the deep shade of the cluster of cottonwoods near the pond.

"Well?" she asked. "What is it? I've got a lot of work to do today."

He jerked his chin toward the barn. "Yeah, I can see."

Maggie turned away. "You can see yourself out."

"When I heard you'd brought that drifter home, I figured you were looking to fill some lonely hours. Don't tell me you've actually hired him."

His words stopped her. "You heard what?"

"Oh, come on, Maggie. You know what a small town Destiny is. It doesn't take more than a whiff of something nasty to start the local rumor mill."

Yes, she knew better than most. Two years ago, Alan had walked out on their ten-year marriage, their daughter and the ranch after realizing he'd never get total ownership of the Crescent Moon. The news kept the town buzzing for months. Had someone seen her and Landon last night in the parking lot before Willie'd shown up?

"You stopped by to gossip?"

Kyle closed the gap between them, pulling off his Stetson. "No. I came for two reasons. The first is to apologize for last night."

Suspicious, Maggie stepped back. In the two years since Alan had headed for greener pastures, Kyle had tried everything to get to her. She'd fallen for it until she discovered the devious snake coiled behind his charismatic smile.

"Fine," she replied, borrowing Landon's word.

"Good. The second is you left before the big announcement. I thought it was best you heard it from me."

She had no idea what Kyle was talking about. She eyed his western-cut suit and shiny cowboy boots with barely a scratch on them. The whole outfit probably cost more than what she'd paid in vet fees for the last six months.

"Don't tell me." She offered a phony smile. "You're selling your holdings and leaving town?"

A grin pulled into a deep dimple. "No. As of this morning I'm the newest board member at Destiny's First National Bank."

Her world shifted. It took all Maggie's strength not to close her eyes. Kyle Greeley a board member at her bank? With his influence, he might as well own it. Like he now owned her ass.

The gleam in his blue eyes, tinged red from partying last night, had her wanting to slap the patronizing look off his face.

"I understand you have a meeting later this week with the branch manager." Kyle twirled his hat in his hands. "About rolling the balloon payment on your loan into extended financing?"

This time her world completely stopped. The air stilled, every sound vanished and it was impossible to catch her breath. She forced the words from her mouth, praying she wouldn't choke on them. "What about it?"

"It's been cancelled. I don't think the bank can afford to…" His voice trailed off as he looked around, his gaze stopping to rest on each of the buildings.

Maggie followed his pointed look, seeing her home as he did. Run-down, the list of needed repairs, both seen and unseen, too numerous to count.

"…take a chance on such a risky operation as the Moon," he finished. "My fellow board members agree."

"You son of a bitch." Maggie's voice was low. Anger fueled her defense of the land that had been in her family for generations. "You know how great the Moon was, and can be again. That's why you're so desperate to get your greedy hands on it."

"You sound like the desperate one here."

"Bull—" Maggie cut off her reply when her grandmother appeared with another basket of wet laundry and Maggie's straw cowboy hat sitting on top. "Nana, look who stopped by for a visit."

"Yes, I see. Hello, Kyle." The older woman wrinkled her nose in Kyle's direction. "My, you're looking more like your daddy every day. I'd add 'God, rest his soul,' but as you know, there's been some debate as to which way your pappy headed after he passed on."

Kyle's mouth thinned. "Hello, Ms. Travers. I see your tongue's as sharp as ever."

Nana B. turned her back on Kyle and nudged the basket in Maggie's direction. "You forget something?"

"Obviously." Maggie grabbed her hat and stilled at the sight of the cell phone lying underneath. She never left the house without either one. Until this morning. She caught the mischievous twinkle in her grandmother's eye and slapped her hat on her head. "Don't say a word."

The crunch of tires against gravel filled the air. Maggie watched a metallic-red, four-door pickup with a matching trailer pull into the drive. She could make out Will Harding, the mayor of Destiny, in the passenger seat.

"Honey, I forgot to tell you the mayor called when you were in the shower," Nana B. said. "He said he'd be out this morning instead of Tuesday."

Great. Black Jack had arrived. And none too happy about it by the banging on the sides of the trailer.

"What's Harding doing here?" Kyle said. "Sounds like a pretty unhappy animal. You aren't trying your silly hocus-pocus stuff, are you?"

Kyle's question reminded Maggie he was still there. Locking away her panic at the cancellation of her meeting with the bank manager, she focused on the horse. Right now, her entire future lay inside the trailer.

"That's none of your concern," she said, silently rearranging her to-do list. She'd have to ask Nana B. to pick up Anna.

Dammit, she wasn't ready for this. Despite Landon taking care of the corral, she'd hoped for a day or two to mentally prepare for the volatile horse. But at least the first installment of her fee would be in her bank account this morning. It wasn't enough to pay off the loan, but once word got out about her success with the horse, she was sure more offers would come.

"I'll go over and say my hellos while you finish here," Nana B. said. "Good thing Landon got busy this morning and fixed the corral, isn't it?"

"You actually hired that cowboy? Are you crazy?" Kyle demanded after Nana B. left. "You know I fired him last night."

Maggie noticed the trailer stop shaking when the truck halted. A good sign? Or was Black Jack resting before round two?

She refocused on Kyle. "I was there, remember? And who I hire is none of your business."

"Well, I do have half interest in this land—"

"Wrong. If I don't make the last payment on my loan, the *bank* gets half interest. But that's not going to happen. This ranch is going to be one hundred percent mine. I want it all."

"You're getting it all, thanks to that cowboy. Cartwright sure is making himself at home. Hell, I tried for months and never got invited back here."

No, he hadn't. In the midst of the pain and disillusionment of her divorce, Maggie never had the desire to be intimate with Kyle. Thanks to Alan's extramarital activities the last few years, she'd had no desire to be physically close to any man.

Unlike last night when a total stranger had kissed her—a kiss she'd started to participate in—before he'd pulled away. And thanks to a not-so-subtle nudge from his horse, it looked as if Landon had intended on a repeat performance.

Did that mean he remembered what happened last night?

Maggie yanked the brim of her hat low over her eyes. "I think it's time you left."

"You sure do rile easily." Kyle trailed the back of his hand down her bare arm. "Maybe I was too quick to accept Alan's word you were an ice queen. Makes me wonder what it'd be like to see you fired up—"

She shook off his touch, disgust filling her. "Goodbye, Kyle."

"I'll see you again…soon."

Maggie propped her hands on her hips and waited until he climbed into his glossy, oversized pickup. Pulling in a deep breath, she looked up at the bright-blue sky, and blew it out. Straightening, she adjusted her hat then froze. Landon had stepped from the barn, and was staring at her. He turned and headed for her visitors.

What the hell was he doing?

She started toward him as he shook hands with the mayor. Quickening her pace, Maggie forced a confident grin and said a quick prayer. She hoped that's all she would need. The last thing she wanted was Kyle's disparaging hocus-pocus comment, or the memory of her father and ex-husband sharing the same sentiment, getting inside her head.

"Good morning, Will." She greeted the mayor with a handshake. "Good to see you."

"You, too, Maggie," he replied. "What was Greeley doing here?"

"He stopped on his way into town." Maggie raised her voice over the ruckus Black Jack created inside the trailer. She had to get these men away from the horse for this to work. "I must say that was quite a celebration yesterday."

Will Harding's chest puffed up at the praise, as Maggie knew it would. "I think it was the best Fourth of July we've had in years," she continued, backing away from the rocking trailer. She looked over her shoulder, caught Landon's gaze and tipped her head toward the house. A puzzled look came over his features, but he, too, backed away.

She focused again on Will. "You were right to bring in more rides for the younger crowd. The kids stuck around instead of going off and getting into trouble like teenagers tend to do—"

"Don't you want to get the horse out of there?" Will asked, jerking his thumb over his shoulder.

"All in good time." Maggie maneuvered the group until they reached the grassy area surrounding the house. "Why don't you go inside and get some coffee? I think Nana B. has some cranberry muffins cooling in the kitchen."

"How long is this going to take, Maggie?" He glanced at his watch. "I've got a late-morning meeting. Your cowboy was about to get a rope—"

"I think Black Jack is a bit upset," Maggie interrupted with what she hoped was a reassuring smile. "Let's give him a few minutes to calm down."

Calm down?

Landon looked at the shaking trailer. Hell, if the horse kicked any harder it was going to topple the damn thing over. Anger radiated from the vehicle and hung in the air like a dark thundercloud ready to explode. Much like his new boss as she glared at him from beneath her straw cowboy hat.

Curiosity at the sound of an approaching vehicle had had Landon stepping from the barn, but the sight of Greeley standing close to Maggie had started a low burn in his gut. The rush of annoyance had surprised him, and he'd quickly doused it with a hefty dose of common sense.

What'd happened earlier was him thinking purely with the lower part of his anatomy. Not a mistake he'd make again. She was his boss, for the time being at least, and he needed to keep his hands, and his thoughts, to himself.

"Kyle told me I was nuts to recommend you for this." The mayor, built more like a pro wrestler than a politician, followed Maggie onto the porch. His words pulled Landon from his thoughts. "If you hadn't done such a great job with that beast of Trish's…"

Landon watched Maggie's smile slip. Was this guy going to give her a hard time, too? He moved to stand behind her. She took a deep breath and relaxed her shoulders. Good girl.

"Working with your daughter's horse was a challenge, but with a great outcome," she replied, "that's why Tucker Hargrove hired me to work with Black Jack."

"Well, that and my wife really talked you up to him. Did I tell you he's looking to build a home near Destiny? He's still a real cowboy despite just playing one in the movies for the last two decades."

"Which is why I want him to have the best horse—"

"Black Jack is the best," Will interrupted.

"Not if he can't be ridden. Hargrove's daughter has been riding since she was a child, but a teenager needs an animal she can handle. A horse she can teach, as well as learn from."

"And you've got a magic spell that'll turn an ornery creature into a winner?" Will asked.

"Yes."

Landon heard the assurance in her voice, but the second of indecision before she spoke kicked his trainer senses into full gear. He closed the distance between them. "You need any help?"

"No." Maggie looked at him, her smile more natural and easy now. "Not at the moment, thanks."

Nana B. opened the back door and took over occupying the mayor with chatty conversation. Within minutes, she herded them inside. Maggie sighed in relief, then headed for the trailer.

"Hey, wait a minute—"

"Back off, cowboy." She whirled toward him, but continued walking backwards. "I know what I'm doing."

Landon followed as far as the end of his truck and stopped. He doubted she was crazy enough to open the trailer and let the wild animal loose, but hell—who'd have thought she'd bring him back to her ranch?

She slowed when she approached the vehicle, circling the entire truck and trailer a few times. Then she started to trace a path back and forth from one side of the horse trailer to the other. Landon had no idea what she was doing, but by her third pass, the horse had stopped his persistent banging. Maggie's lips moved, but he couldn't hear what she was saying.

Was she talking to herself? To the horse?

He braced his hands on his hips and shifted his weight to one foot. The desire to go to her remained powerful. Then it merged with confusion as to why. Both battled inside his head while he watched her.

She retraced her steps, moving closer to the vehicle each time until she paused on the side facing him. She slowly leaned against the trailer, crossed her arms over her chest and bent her head as if studying the ground, not moving.

Landon checked his watch. Fifteen minutes later, she waved him over. He followed her hand signals to take a wide berth. She moved in the same direction, but stayed closer, her hand gliding along the trailer's smooth surface.

She motioned him toward the pickup. "Start it up." Her voice was low and soothing. "Can you maneuver this thing back to the main corral?"

He nodded.

"Good. Go slow and easy and no matter what, don't stop," she said. "I'll be where you can see me in the side mirror."

Climbing into the pickup, Landon settled behind the wheel and cranked over the engine. He glanced in the mirror. Maggie continued to talk, but he was too far away to hear her. He inched the truck into reverse, using both side mirrors to guide him and keep an eye on the backside of a certain lady rancher. A very nice backside.

"Keep your mind on your work," Landon muttered to himself, focusing his eyes somewhere else.

He got the vehicle in place and shut off the engine. Exiting the cab, he took the same wide circle as he headed for the corral. The lilting tone of Maggie's voice called to him and he watched her open the main gate. The trailer was still ten feet from the opening. They'd have to move it back farther.

She must have read his mind and shook her head. He opened his mouth to protest, but she waved him off. Somehow, she'd gotten the horse quiet again, but there was no telling how the animal would react once the trailer's gate opened. He took a step toward her, but she glared at him.

Damn, she was crazy! He went to his truck, grabbed a length of rope and fashioned it into a lasso.

"Trust her, Landon. She knows what she's doing."

Nana B. and the mayor stood on the porch. How long had they been there?

"It's the horse I don't trust," he said.

"Smart move," Will said. "It took four men to get the damn thing into the trailer. Don't tell me she's going to—"

"Not by herself, she's not." Landon rolled his shoulders and headed to the far side of the trailer.

He wished his muscles were less sore, but no matter. He heard the bolt slide and the creaking of the gate. Rounding the corner, he found Maggie lowering the ramp to the ground. She looked his way, her gaze climbing the length of him. He planted his feet, the rope hanging loose in his hands. He could see in her eyes she wanted him to leave.

No way.

She frowned and turned her attention back to the trailer. Landon didn't know if she was accepting his defiance or not.

He didn't care.

"Okay, boy, you're free." Her voice remained calm as she spoke to the horse, who, except for pawing at the metal flooring and a swish of his tail, remained quiet. "Now, I want you to back out of there and follow me straight into the corral. You hear me, Black Jack?"

She had to be kidding.

Landon fought the urge to roll his eyes, and instead concentrated on the horse's first step. Maggie repeated the commands as the mustang slowly emerged. The animal remained peaceful as it followed her inside the corral, stopping in the center. She stepped out of its way and scooted outside the fence.

"You can burn off some of that energy now," Maggie called after firmly closing the gate.

The horse responded with a loud whinny and a toss of his head before he galloped with wild abandon around the enclosed pen.

Awe rippled through Landon. "Hands down, that is the most amazing thing I've ever seen."

"Thank you." She didn't look at him, but continued to stare at the horse. "You can put your rope away and move the truck."

He did as he was told. The mayor headed out, looking a bit shell-shocked and Nana B. returned to the house. Landon watched Maggie talk to the still-nervous horse. He'd been around animals all his life and he'd never seen anyone handle a horse, especially one with such a surly disposition, the way Maggie had.

Before he could start toward her, Nana B. appeared with his clothes neatly folded and stacked. "This is the first bunch. You got more coming."

"I appreciate you doing this." Landon opened the driver's side door and reached for his empty duffel bag.

Nana B. nudged him out of the way and deposited the stack into the open canvas bag. "Why don't you let your horse get some fresh air, before you load him inside your trailer?"

Landon just nodded in reply, having already decided it was Maggie's place as ranch owner to let her family know she'd hired him, at least temporarily.

He waited until Nana B. headed back inside. He kept his back to the open cab of his truck, then yanked the Crescent Moon ranch shirt over his head without bothering to undo the buttons. He grabbed a light blue T-shirt and pulled it on, tucking the hem into his jeans while he walked.

When he reached the corral, he copied Maggie's posture with one foot on the bottom rung of the fence. His elbows rested next to hers on the top railing, and he eyed the midnight-black horse prancing back and forth inside the corral.

"He's a beauty, isn't he?" she said.

Her soft words invited him to look at her. "A beauty and a beast rolled into one. I can't figure out how you got him to walk out of the trailer."

"All I did was give Black Jack time to relax, get used to the smells of his new surroundings and one person to focus on." She bumped up the brim of her cowboy hat and smiled. "I also threw in a bit of mag…"

Her voice trailed off and her eyes widened, skimming over his chest and shoulders. His skin grew hot under the intensity of her stare. A desperate need to know what was going on inside her pretty head filled him, but he pushed it away.

"A bit of what?"

"I'm sorry?"

"You were telling me how you got the horse to listen."

"Oh, ah…" Maggie's smile came back, full and natural. "A bit of magic."

"I don't believe in magic," he said.

"Well, I guess I'll have a chance to change your mind."

Landon opened his mouth to protest, but Maggie pushed on. "Oh, I know you're probably a man who sets his mind to something and that's that. My other cowboys thought the same, too, but I converted them."

"Then they walked out on you?"

Maggie's smile faded. A warm breeze caught the end of her ponytail and chased it into her face. "Which is why I'm looking for more help. Willie and Hank are the best and have been here forever, but they can't handle the work alone."

He nodded. "I wondered why it was so quiet."

"When you interrupted me and Greeley last night…well, he'd just hired away my last two hands." The smooth column of her throat rippled as she swallowed before turning back to watch the horse. "Something he's been real good at over the last six months."

The image of her and Greeley flashed in his head again. "Why?"

"That's another story—" she stopped and pushed out a deep breath "—for another time. Look, we didn't talk about pay. It's not much, but it includes feed and board for your horse. Thanks to Nana B., the food for us humans is good, too." She pointed to the far side of the yard, past the pond. "The foreman's cabin is empty if you prefer privacy."

Landon glanced over at the structure. "You haven't had a chance to talk to your family about me. Maybe you should clear things with them first—"

She cut him off. "I make all the hiring decisions around here.

Not my grandmother or my cowboys. Not even my daughter, okay?"

"Who?"

"My daughter, Anna."

Maggie's words barely registered as Landon's world spiraled into numb, bitter darkness. Memories charged him and he was powerless to fight them off.

Memories of *his* daughter, Sara.

Of the day he'd entered the nursery in the predawn hours, drawn by her soft cries. Tiny hands outstretched and big tears clinging to her dark lashes, she'd leaned against the railing of her crib. After he'd changed her diaper and warmed a bottle, he'd held her as she ate. Once she'd fallen asleep again, he'd placed her back in the crib, and watched her small chest rise and fall in a steady motion.

"I'll always be here for you, little one," he whispered. "I know I wasn't for a while. I blamed you for the mistakes your mother and I made. I was wrong. But I'm making things better now. You can count on me."

He'd lied to his daughter that day. He hadn't been there for her. He'd had back-to-back meetings all day, and it was dark before he'd returned to the ranch. A mile from the main house, he'd seen a deep orange-and-red glow over the treetops. His foot had stomped the car's accelerator. He'd arrived to find the main barn engulfed, his brother and the ranch hands desperately trying to save the horses and the rest of the outer buildings. He'd joined them, but no one realized the fire had spread to the main house where Sara and her mother were trapped—

"Landon? Landon, are you all right?"

He jerked from the warmth of Maggie's touch, unable to escape the stench of burnt wood or the feel of hungry flames licking at his skin. Reminders of his own private hell. A hell he visited repeatedly in his dreams. A hell that had branded him a murderer.

"My God, what is it? What's wrong?"

"Nothing." Struggling to catch his breath, Landon forced air to move in and out of his lungs. Staring straight ahead, he pushed away the memories and locked them into the dark recesses of his heart. "Leave me alone."

"You're as white as a sheet. What did I say?"

"You didn't—it has nothing to do with—" Landon clenched his jaw so hard his teeth ached. "Please, Maggie, let it go."

"Can I help—"

The walkie-talkie anchored at her hip crackled to life. "Crescent Moon, this is Willie…come in, Maggie."

Maggie's eyes flew from him to the radio and back again.

"Come in, Moon, Willie here. Darn it, girl, where are you?"

"Answer your cowboy," Landon said.

Grabbing her radio, Maggie never broke eye contact as she brought it to her lips. "This is Maggie, what's up, Willie?"

"It's 'bout time. We got ourselves a mess. The front end of Hank's wagon came off the lift."

Confusion filled her eyes. "Can't he wait until after lunch for help?"

"Darlin', Hank's under the wagon."

Chapter Six

Maggie yelled for her grandmother and bolted for the house, Landon close behind. From the moment she'd brought him home, it had seemed as if he was never far away—except for a few moments ago when he'd been lost in a different world. The look of utter misery on his face was heart-wrenching.

Nana B. rushed outside. Maggie filled her in on Willie's call. "We're heading out. Call Doc Cody and ask him to meet us there."

"He's gonna bring that darn ambulance," Nana B. said. "You know Hank isn't going anywhere near it, much less the clinic."

"He might not have a choice this time." Maggie's heart hitched in her chest. She couldn't lose Hank. A quick prayer raced through her before she returned her attention to the walkie-talkie. "Willie…we're on our way."

"Copy that. Got a piece of railing jammed in there for leverage, but I gotta drop this gosh-darn contraption before I drop the railing."

"We'll be there in ten minutes. Don't do anything foolish."

Maggie whirled around, and froze. Damn! Her truck was still in town. She held out her hand to Landon. "Give me your keys."

He ignored her request. Instead, he jumped into his pickup and cranked the engine. "Get in. You told Willie *we* were coming."

Had she? She was so used to using the singular *I* it didn't seem possible she'd have automatically included him. Maggie marched over to the open door. "Move over, I'm driving."

"I can drive."

"I know where I'm going and you're arguing with your boss."

He slid across the seat and Maggie jumped in. Slamming the door shut, she threw the truck into gear and tore out of the driveway. Cutting between the barn and the foreman's cabin, she headed across the open field. Landon braced one hand against the dash when she swung onto a dirt road, never touching the brakes.

"What did you mean when you told your grandmother Hank might not have a choice about the ambulance this time?"

Maggie kept her eyes glued to the wide expanse of land ahead. "Hank's been hurt a lot over the years. Life of a cowboy, I guess. Sometimes we take care of it, sometimes we call the doc. I think Hank would rather fight the devil himself than see the inside of an ambulance."

Her fingers tightened on the steering wheel. "Meredith, Hank's wife, fell sick one winter. I was young, I don't remember her." A lump formed in Maggie's throat, but she pushed her words past it. "I'm told she refused to see a doctor. A storm had dumped a couple feet of snow by the time Hank convinced her to get medical attention. It took the ambulance two hours to get there. She died on the way to the hospital."

Maggie glanced at Landon. His face could have been made of stone for all the emotion he displayed.

"I can see how that would change a man."

"It's been twenty-five years and Hank's never found anyone

new. He used to say he's not likely to find love again. Can you imagine feeling like that about someone?"

"No."

Her eyes flickered to rest on him for a few seconds and she again noted how he was no longer wearing the ranch shirt. It'd shocked her when she'd found him in the faded, denim button-down at breakfast. The sight brought back a powerful and hated memory with such force she'd tripped over her own feet to get away.

Her father had loved those shirts. She'd hated them.

She focused her attention back on the dirt road. A small cabin and barn appeared on the other side of a hill. Maggie stopped in front of the barn. "Willie!" she threw the truck into park and jumped out at the same time. "Where are you?"

"In here," came the muffled reply from deep inside.

Maggie and Landon raced into the cool interior in time to hear the cry of splitting wood and a string of colorful curses. Willie's lips were pulled back from his teeth and cords stood out in his neck and arms. With all his weight on one end of a long wooden lever jammed under the end of the wagon, he'd managed to keep it off Hank's chest long enough for the man to breathe.

Another crack from the railing propelled Landon forward. He maneuvered backward under the wagon, feet on either side of Hank's chest. Bracing his hands on his knees, he took the wagon's full weight on his back as the railing split.

"Hank!"

"Landon!"

Willie and Maggie called out when the wagon fell on Landon. His knees gave a few inches, but he pushed upward, creating space over the fallen cowboy. He closed his eyes. "Get Hank out…now."

Maggie crouched on one side of her cowboy and Willie did the same. They pulled him out of harm's way.

"Willie, grab—hay bales and drag—" Landon grunted the words through clenched teeth "—drag them—"

"Gotcha." Willie grabbed a set of metal bale hooks, dragged the hay and shoved them under the corner of the wagon, kicking aside pieces of the now-useless wooden wheel.

"Let it go, Landon," Maggie begged, "before you get hurt."

Landon's gaze crashed into hers and held for a moment, then he dropped to all fours, his knees hitting the dirt as his Stetson fell from his head. The wagon rested on the makeshift jack created by the bales of hay.

Maggie forced her attention from Landon to Hank. Willie crouched beside him, checking him out. Relief filled her chest when he offered a quick nod of assurance he was okay. "Hank Jarvis! You should be ashamed of yourself. Why in God's name did you get under the wagon?"

"You know why," Hank whispered, his eyes closed against the obvious pain wracking his beefy body. "A promise is—"

"A promise." Maggie cut him off, knowing Hank was talking about the promise he'd made to his wife, when she was on her deathbed, to fully restore the antique Texas buckboard wagon they'd bought together. A promise that had taken a quarter of a century to keep. "I can't lose you, too, Hank. I can't."

"I'm not going anywhere, honey." Hank opened his eyes. "It's a couple of bruised ribs."

"You're probably right." Willie rose to his feet. "You need checking out all the same. We should call Doc—"

"Maggie, come in, Maggie." The walkie-talkie again came to life, this time with Nana B.'s voice coming over the airwaves.

Maggie pressed the talk button. "He's okay. We got here in time."

"Saints be praised! Doc's out at the McIntire place. He's on his way."

Landon moved out from beneath the wagon. "Tell her we'll

meet them at the house." Waving off Willie's outstretched hand, he rose to his feet and grabbed his hat. He placed it back on his head and brushed off his clothes. "Hank should stay flat. We can put him in the truck bed. I'll bring it around."

Landon headed out of the barn, walking stiffly, but not limping. She couldn't believe what he'd done. "Nana, we're bringing Hank in. Have Doc meet us there."

"I heard," her grandmother said. "I'll be waiting."

"I'll get some blankets." Willie ran out behind Landon.

Maggie's gaze went back to Hank, air pinching in her chest at the pain etched on his weathered face. My God, if they hadn't gotten here in time. If Landon hadn't been with her—

His truck appeared inside the barn doors. Willie returned and jumped in the back, arranging a makeshift bed. Landon got out and moved toward them. The brim of his hat was pulled so low Maggie couldn't see his face. It struck her he always wore it that way.

"Ready to move him?" he asked.

"I'm hurt," Hank groused, "not dead."

"Lay still, you stubborn fool," Maggie said.

"This'll work a lot easier if you don't help," Landon said to Hank, sliding his hands under the cowboy's shoulder and hips. Maggie followed suit on her side while Willie supported his friend's legs. "On three…"

Muscles flexing in his arms and shoulders, Landon took the majority of Hank's weight. They put the cowboy in the truck bed, his boots hanging off the tailgate and his face three shades paler than before.

"You stay with him." Landon started for the cab. "I'll drive."

Maggie grabbed his forearm. "Can you drive? Are you hurt, too?"

"I'm fine."

He tried to pull away but she held on. "First the corral and now this. All I keep saying is 'thank you.'"

His dark eyes focused on her for a long moment before he nodded and stepped back. She released him and sat next to Hank. Willie joined Landon in the truck. They headed back to the main house and found Nana B. pacing in the driveway.

Willie jumped out after Landon parked. "Need bandages for his ribs," he told them. "If the doc wants to take him in, it's gonna be a long ride to town."

"I ain't going."

"Oh, pipe down, old man." Nana B. hovered nearby.

"Hank, please." Maggie looked at the man who was more a father to her than the man who'd raised her. "How about I take you in the truck? Will you go if I drive?"

"Is it…necessary?" Hank breathed.

"If you ever plan on getting back on a horse, it is," Landon said, moving toward them.

Maggie's gaze collided with his, seeing the gravity in his eyes. Was he right, or only saying that to scare Hank into getting help? The thought of Hank never being able to ride again tore at her.

Willie returned and climbed up next to Maggie with the bandages. "I see our newest boarder is here. Isn't Black Jack a bit early?"

Hank tried to sit up. "That wild horse is here? You shouldn't have taken him on all alone—"

"Lie still," Maggie ordered when Hank winced in pain. "I—ah, we took care of him."

"Let's get these thingamajiggers on you." Willie held up the bandages.

"Here, let me help." Landon gestured at her. "You need to get out of there. Not enough room for all of us."

"But your back—"

"I told you I'm fine." His response was as firm as his touch when he reached for her.

Maggie grabbed his hand, her pulse racing as she allowed

him to help her down. She moved to stand next to her grand-mother as Landon climbed in.

"I'm not made of glass you know," Hank grumbled. "I won't break."

"You're already broken," Nana B. shot back, her hands tightly wringing. "How did this happen?"

Maggie filled her in, her eyes drawn to Landon as he crouched behind Hank's shoulders and lifted. Willie worked quickly, wrapping ace bandages right over Hank's shirt.

"And if Landon hadn't taken the weight of that old wagon on his back the moment the lever gave way…" Maggie paused, emotion clogging her throat, "I don't know what would've happened. We could have lost—"

"It's all right, Magpie," Hank said, using her childhood nickname. "I might be useless for a while, but I'm not ready to punch my ticket to the pearly gates yet."

Useless for a while…*ohmigod, what was she going to do now?*

Maggie's fear transformed into panic. The sharp sting of tears bit at her eyes. Hank would be out of commission for at least a few weeks, and Landon only planned to stick around the same length of time. Her help-wanted ads flashed through her mind, the word "wanted" morphing into "desperate" with a capital *D*.

"I should've known better." Hank's face contorted in pain as Willie continued to work. "I heard about those two losers walking on us. Maybe—damn, that hurts—ah, we have about a million miles of fence line to deal with, and I'm gonna be laid up like a fat bass at a fishing tournament. Maybe you should talk to Greeley about borrowing help—"

"No!" Maggie bit hard at her bottom lip to stop her outburst. She jammed her hands into the back pockets of her jeans, eyes glued to the ground. "I can handle it."

"We can handle it."

Her head jerked up at Landon's words to find him staring at her.

"Maybe you should tell them."

Maggie saw resignation mixed with torment in his eyes before he looked away. He didn't want to work here. When he'd offered to take the job she thought she'd seen something—familiarity, acceptance—in the dark depths of his eyes. And after her work with Black Jack, she'd reveled in the respect she'd read there.

However, when she'd started talking about the job, assuring him she did all the hiring at the Crescent Moon, an expression of such desperation and pain came over his face it'd astounded her.

She realized four pairs of eyes were staring at her. "Ah, Landon's offered to stick around for a while. His horse is laid up and he's agreed to work for a few weeks until G.W. is better. Or until I hire more help."

The shock on Willie's face and her grandmother's pleased expression didn't surprise her. Hank's expression was a mix of confusion and pain, but he held out his hand to Landon.

"Thanks for sticking around, and for saving me back there."

An overwhelming need to repeat her cowboy's gratitude filled Maggie as Landon shook Hank's hand. She spun away, needing to put some distance between herself and the truck before the words spilled from her mouth.

What was the matter with her?

Landon was simply another cowboy, not the second coming of her salvation. Or her sex life. So, okay, she was attracted to the man, but she had more important things to worry about than kisses and—

"Do you still want me?"

His heated words caressed the side of her face. Maggie whirled, her face flaming. "Yes, I want—ah, yes of course, you're hired. Are you sure you're okay? You didn't hurt yourself?"

He squared his shoulders and took a step back. "Aren't you getting tired of asking me that?"

A white SUV spun into the yard, stopping Maggie from answering him. Seconds later, a little girl with braids raced across the gravel driveway.

"Mama! What happened? Are you all right?"

"I'm okay, sweetie." Maggie drew her daughter into a long hug, breathing in her sweet smell. Doc Cody got out of the truck and headed their way. "Thanks for coming, Doc. What's Anna doing with you?"

"Julie's mom heard in town about your call for help. Anna insisted on coming home. I ran into them at the crossroads and offered to bring her the rest of the way."

Maggie nodded, knowing the call must have frightened her daughter. She put her arm around Anna's shoulders and gave a quick squeeze. "Sweetie, everything's okay. Hank got knocked around a bit—"

"Hank!" The little girl wrenched free and ran to the back of the truck. "What happened? What did you do?"

"I'm—I'm fine, Little Bit," Hank whispered, lifting his head to look toward her. "Don't worry about me."

Anna looked at Maggie with wide, trusting eyes. "Is he gonna be all right?"

"Yes, Anna, he is." She ran her hand along her daughter's blond hair, giving a small tug on the end of a braid. She pulled her away from the doctor, who was already speaking with Hank. "And we have someone special to thank for saving Hank. I want you to meet our new cowboy, Landon Cartwright."

She didn't think it was possible, but he'd tugged his Stetson even lower on his brow. His hands braced on his hips, fingers spread wide and digging hard into the denim of his jeans.

"Landon, I'd like you to meet my daughter, Anna." Maggie wondered if he was in more pain than he was letting on with his rigid posture. "Anna, this is the man who saved Hank's life."

Landon opened his mouth as if to protest, but before he

could say a word, Anna flew at him and wrapped her arms around his middle.

"Oh, thank you! Thank you!"

"Gotta admit this is a good idea, camping out to deal with the fence line repairs."

Landon glanced over at Willie. The old man continued to look straight ahead, his thin frame rocking naturally with the movement of his horse.

They'd left the main house a half hour ago, each on horseback, with enough supplies to last at least a week.

Maggie had convinced Hank to go to the hospital after all. He'd be home later and staying at the main house while he nursed what the doctor had figured was four cracked ribs.

With Hank on bed rest for the unforeseeable future, Willie filled Landon in on his and Hank's daily trips to repair the broken fence line. Camping out instead of returning back to the main house was something Landon had used at his own ranch in the past.

And it would keep him away from a certain little girl and her mother.

"Course, that leaves the womenfolk with just Hank to look out for 'em," Willie continued. "No matter. Laid up or not, he's still a pretty good shot."

Landon eyed the shotgun holstered on the side of Willie's saddle. "Is there a reason he needs to be?"

The old cowboy didn't answer him, but said instead, "I take it sweet little girls ain't your cup of tea?"

"What are you talking about?"

"Saw the look on your face when Miss Anna wrapped you in a bear hug." The old cowboy cackled like a wet hen. "Would've thought someone had come at you with a red-hot branding iron."

Landon tugged on his Stetson. Damn! At this rate, he was going to punch his head right through the top of it. He shifted, trying to get used to the new mount he reluctantly accepted, as G.W. was in no shape to be involved in ranch work.

The memory of the little girl's arms wrapped around his middle stuck with him long after Maggie, face flushed with embarrassment, peeled her daughter away. Four years since his daughter's death. In the nine months since his release from prison, he'd taken great pains to stay far away from children.

Finding out Maggie had a child, and the flashback to the night he'd lost his own baby girl, was a blow he still hadn't recovered from.

"She surprised me, is all," he said.

"Yeah, I figured." Willie removed his hat and wiped at his face with a faded bandanna. "Mind if we stop by Hank's place first? We flew out of there like our tail feathers were burning. Wanna make sure things are locked up tight."

"More problems with your neighbor, Greeley?"

Willie's head snapped around, his gaze sharp. "What makes you ask?"

Landon quickly filled Willie in on the man's visit to the ranch earlier. "It doesn't take a rocket scientist to figure out he sees this place as easy pickings."

When they arrived at Hank's cabin, he stopped his horse next to Willie's. Both men dismounted.

"Other than stealing her cowboys, what else is Greeley doing?" Landon asked.

"You struck me as a person who minded his own business."

"Look, old man, I work here now." Landon admired Willie's loyalty, but he refused to be kept in the dark. "Part of my job is looking out for our boss and this ranch. Like you said, I didn't get jumped last night for nothing."

Willie nodded, but remained quiet as he went inside the cabin. Moments later, he closed the door behind him, double-checking to make sure it was secure. He returned to Landon and the horses. "Let's check out the barn."

Landon followed.

"Maggie's daddy died five years ago. A bastard to the end, he left half interest of the Moon to that sorry excuse for a husband of hers." Willie's gravelly voice filled the interior as he checked each stall on one side of the barn. "When Alan Stevens walked a few years back, Maggie bought him out."

"You mind telling me what we're looking for?" Landon asked, grateful the old man was talking, but not sure how Maggie's father and ex-husband played into what was going on with her neighbor.

"Anything that looks like it doesn't belong."

"I guess that makes sense." Landon mirrored Willie's actions, but neither of them found anything out of place.

"Gonna check the loft." Willie headed for the front end of the barn.

Landon walked to the center and stood next to the wagon on the hay bales. "What else is going on?"

"Well, ranching is a dying art. Nowadays, it's about dollars and cents instead of cattle, cowboys and common sense." Willie's voice echoed from the loft. "The ways that blowhard ex of Maggie's handled the books barely left us breathing. Now, she's trying to keep all our heads above the rising waters. Thanks to equipment failing or disappearing, cowboys walking and damage to the fence line no one's got a good explanation for, we're busier than a one-legged man in a butt-kickin' contest."

Landon shook his head at Willie's analogy. "And you think Greeley's responsible?"

"Well, like you said, the slimy weasel's got his eye on this place."

"Isn't his ranch, the Triple G, the biggest in the county?"

"Sure is. In fact, it butts up against our land on the east. That's a section of fence line that never has any problems."

Landon nudged at the broken pieces of a shattered wagon wheel with the toe of his boot, his gaze falling on the smooth edges of what he figured were the spokes. Dropping to a crouch, he studied them. "Hey, Willie?"

"Yeah?"

"How did Hank get stuck under the wagon?"

"He said he was attaching the wheels, but something must've gone wrong." Willie left the loft and joined him in the center of the barn. "Why?"

"Look at these pieces. When wood breaks, it splinters. The edges on these pieces are smooth, as if they were cut."

"Well, I'll be a suck-egg mule." Willie rose and scurried toward the barn doors.

"Where are you going?" Landon said.

"To call the sheriff. This is gonna stop right here and now."

Chapter Seven

Landon eased himself into the claw-footed tub. A moan of appreciation for the hot water on his aching muscles rushed past his lips.

Working two weeks straight on the fence line had meant camping out nightly beneath the stars with Willie. It also meant washing up in an ice-cold stream. Despite daily temperatures in the nineties, those encounters had grown old quickly. He'd dealt with downed barbed wire plenty of times in the past, and he and Willie fell into an easy teamwork pattern of repositioning the posts and restringing the wire. The last pole this morning had caused the familiar shooting pain to rip right through him. Thankfully, the throbbing receded as he and Willie had ridden back.

They arrived around suppertime to find only Nana B. and Hank at the main house. Willie asked if there'd been any trouble. Nana B. assured him things had been quiet, with nary a sight of Greeley in days. Not wanting to analyze why he was relieved at the news, Landon'd checked on G.W., glad to see his buddy back to form.

Sliding down, he immersed himself completely in the steaming water. He sat up again, shoving his hair back from his face, unable to push Maggie out of his head.

Damn the woman.

Out of sight, out of mind.

That had been his plan for stamping out the tight coil of emotion she'd caused him. It hadn't worked.

He grabbed the soap lying on the shelf next to the tub, and created a sudsy lather. He rubbed at his scars for a moment before letting his eyes close. He leaned against the cool porcelain and let the weariness of two weeks of hard work slowly take over his body. Shutting down his mind wasn't as easy. In order to survive working here, he'd have to stay as far away from Maggie as possible.

If he got the chance to stick around.

His mind flew back to the morning in Hank's barn when Willie was talking to the sheriff on the phone.

The last thing Landon had wanted or needed was to get anywhere near the local law. A wave of shame hit him. A man had been hurt, and if his gut feeling was right, and it usually was, it hadn't been an accident. A deputy sheriff, who looked barely out of high school, showed up. Landon answered as few questions as possible, but didn't flinch when the kid looked him straight in the eye. Neither he nor Willie offered Greeley's name, but Willie did tell the deputy about the ranch's troubles. Then they headed out again with Willie relaying word of the deputy's visit to Maggie. She wasn't happy with the news.

Later that night, and many nights after, Willie had shared more stories about life on the Crescent Moon. Maggie's father had been a bastard, and her ex wasn't much better.

Landon thought about what she'd gone through most of her

life, living with men who did little or nothing to build her self-esteem. The woman he'd come to know, thanks to Willie's nonstop chatter, amazed him. He found himself wanting to work harder, pushing harder to get the job done, and done right.

For her.

A sudden pounding came at the front door. "Landon! Are you in there?"

Maggie.

"Landon, can you hear me? I need to talk to you and it can't wait."

He looked around and found the towel lying on the bed. He started to rise. "Just a minute," he called out.

The front door slammed open. "Landon! How could you…"

He dropped back, splashing water over the edge of the tub. Muscles tensed as Maggie's wide-eyed gaze roamed over him.

A long minute passed. Her presence filled the one-room cabin. He tried his damnedest to keep his eyes on her face and not the miles of tanned skin displayed by her short denim skirt and sexy, red cowboy boots. It wasn't hard to do with her hair flowing around her shoulders, smoky makeup emphasizing the bright green of her eyes and the red stain on her lips. She looked ready for a night on the town.

A heated emotion slammed into his chest. Jealousy? Whatever the feeling, he squashed it. "Is there something you wanted?" he asked instead.

"You're in the bathtub."

Breaking free of her gaze, Landon stared at the fabric privacy divider standing uselessly at the foot of the tub. "Not much gets by you."

"What are you doing?"

Growing harder by the second. Landon slammed closed the thought and decided to go for the obvious. "Taking a bath."

"Why?"

"Because I'm dirty, tired and I thought it might relax my sore muscles."

Not every sore muscle, pal.

This was the closest they'd been in two weeks. He'd heard her daily over the walkie-talkie he carried, but she'd only spoken to Willie. Her voice had sounded throaty and sexy over the device. It'd stuck with him, haunting his waking hours and his dreams—

He pushed the thought away. Her voice was having the same effect on him right now. He placed his elbows on the tub's edge, using his hands to create a screen between Maggie's gaze and the lower half of his body, despite being chest-deep in soapy water.

Where was his damn hat when he needed it? "Do you mind? It's a bit drafty in here."

Pink stained her cheeks. She stepped inside and slammed the door closed.

He raised an eyebrow. "You're on the wrong side."

"Too bad. I know what you did, Landon." She marched to the edge of the tub. "And I'm pissed as hell."

What in God's name was she talking about? His prison record?

She waved a fistful of papers in his face. "What the hell gave you the right to sell those horses?"

Realization dawned. "I didn't sell them."

"Don't split hairs with me." She crossed her arms under her breasts, pushing them against the snug T-shirt. "I know it was you who called the Still Waters Ranch in Texas."

It'd taken a ten-minute call to his brother's foreman to convince him Maggie's horses would fit in perfectly on the ranch. "Hank made the sale—"

"Hank closed the deal because he has the authority to do so, but neither of us had ever heard of Still Waters. Did you think I would accept this sale as a stroke of good luck without checking into it?"

He should've known she wouldn't. Landon had seen the quality horseflesh his first morning at the ranch, and again when he'd checked on G.W. last week. When Willie said he suspected Greeley was somehow keeping Maggie from getting a good deal in the local market, he'd made the call.

"How are you connected to Still Waters?"

Landon was pulled from his thoughts. "What?"

"I spoke with a Storm Watkins. He told me a former employee contacted them." Maggie again waved the papers. "Then he double-talked his way out of giving any more information."

"You're fishing."

"Is it true? Did you work there?"

Yeah, he'd worked there. Since he'd been able to walk. It was his family's ranch. And except for a few years on the rodeo circuit, right up until the day they'd led him away in handcuffs.

Rippling waves of bath water competed with Landon's rippling muscles for Maggie's attention, but the intensity in his coal-black eyes made it impossible to look anywhere else.

"You haven't answered me. Did you work on the Still Waters Ranch?"

"Does it matter?"

Hell, yes it mattered. When Hank told her about an offer coming from a ranch in Texas, Maggie went from shocked to suspicious in a matter of minutes. At first, she thought Greeley was somehow behind it, conjuring a bogus deal to tie her up in endless paper work. Then a fax arrived with a fair-market amount, a bit over her asking price.

Talking to the ranch's foreman had been like talking to a brick wall, but when she'd threatened to cancel the deal despite the money being wired to her bank, he'd relented enough to tell her the initial contact came from a former employee.

It'd taken all of thirty seconds before she was out the door. It had to be Landon.

She'd spent the last fourteen days convincing herself Landon was another temporary cowboy who'd do his job, collect his paycheck and soon be on his way. Willie's reports of Landon's hard work hadn't surprised her, but his expertise with time-saving techniques on the fence line had.

Now with him arranging this sale, she didn't know what he was up to. Did he think she couldn't handle things here at her own ranch? Could he actually be positioning himself to take over the Moon? Damn, she had enough to deal with when it came to Kyle and her ex-husband. The last thing she needed was another man seeing her as a helpless—

"Hello? Maggie? Cat got your tongue?"

Startled from her thoughts, Maggie focused on Landon and the water beading over his body's hard planes. Soapy water lapped around bent knees, rising and falling over the brown, pebbled nipples on a muscular chest.

She blinked and directed her gaze to the paper work in her hands. "I don't know what you're doing, but taking care of this ranch is my responsibility."

"Who said it wasn't?"

A frustrated sound escaped. "What made you call Still Waters? I didn't see it on the list of references you left with Nana B."

"So? Didn't my former bosses say enough glowing things about me?"

"I don't know. I didn't call them."

A shocked look crossed Landon's face. Maggie kept flipping through the paper work, the printed words nothing more than a blur. "I learned a long time ago to trust my instincts. To listen to the little voice inside my head, inside my heart. It's something I've ignored in the past, and I'm still living with the consequences."

A ragged breath escaped her lungs. The next words popped from her mouth before she could pull them back. "But I trusted you."

Landon sighed and kept his hands in a tight grip over his

chest. "Yes, I worked there. And before you get to the page that lists the owner, I'll tell you right now he's…" His eyes closed. "His name is Chase Cartwright. He's my brother."

Maggie gasped. A look of anguish came over him. Not the intense pain she'd seen two weeks ago, but enough heartache that it squeezed her own heart.

Unable to stop herself, she dropped to a crouch next to the tub and laid one hand over his clenched fingers. His skin was hot and wet. The scent of clean man filled her head as she focused on the impossibly long, dark lashes across his skin. "Landon, what is it?"

He jerked from her touch and opened his eyes, but didn't look at her. "It's nothing." A muscle ticked along his jawline. "It's no big deal."

"It is a big deal." Maggie laid her fingers along his chin, and pressed until he looked at her. "I can see it on your face. Please, let me help—"

An invisible door slammed shut in his eyes, and Landon yanked from her touch. He leaned as far away from her as the tub allowed. "I don't need help."

Her hand fell away and landed on the tight muscles of his arm. "Landon—"

He opened his eyes again, and a flatness, devoid of any emotion, stared at her. "You don't want to sell the horses, fine. I don't give a damn."

"Yes, you do. What I don't understand is why you're doing this—"

"Do you need me to spell it out, Maggie?" Landon's lips creased into a smirk. He grabbed her hand and brought it to his mouth. His lips caressed the back of her hand before tracing the ridge of her knuckles. "I wanted to get into the good graces of my lady boss."

A blaze ignited in her stomach. Much like the one he'd created in the dark interior of his truck when he'd slanted his mouth over hers in a searing kiss. Now, that same mouth sucked at her skin, that same tongue tracked the crevice of her clasped fingers.

"Landon, I don't…"

A storm of fury and lust flared in his eyes. Her heart seized in her chest. Before it jumped back to life again, the emotion in those dark depths vanished.

He lifted his mouth from her hand. "Liar."

She reared back, stumbling as she forced her legs to obey her silent command to move. Was her desire so obvious? Could he see the fantasies that haunted her dreams in her eyes? Humiliation filled her, and she bolted for the door. She grabbed the handle and twisted, but powerful arms shot past her to slam it closed again.

"Maggie, wait."

His deep voice whispered her name and the wet heat of his body surrounded her. A wild craving raced through her veins. Did he bother to grab a towel or was he naked behind her?

She pictured the long length of him pressing into her and bit back a moan. Forcing the words out, she said, "Let me out."

"No."

"You did me a favor with the sale, okay? I'll stay out of your business…" She let her voice fade as embarrassment crept over her.

"Maggie, listen to me," he said with quiet emphasis.

"No!"

He leaned closer, his breath warm against her neck. "Why not?"

"Because I won't play games with you."

"Games?"

"One minute you're looking at me like you want to crawl on top of me, slip inside my skin. The next, you shut down and pretend I don't exist. I won't do it, Landon. Let me out."

"No."

His calm refusal twisted her discomfort into anger. Maggie

spun around. His eyes brimmed with tenderness, and her angry words died in her throat. His hair hung around his face, droplets of water falling from it, dampening the front of her shirt.

The tenderness in his gaze melted into the raw yearning she'd seen earlier. The change matched her own battling emotions. How could he look at her this way? Make her feel this way?

"This isn't right." Her words were halfhearted.

"I know."

She raised her hands to push him away, but he captured her wrists in his strong grip and pulled them over her head, gently shackling them against the door. She closed her eyes to hide the desire spinning through her. He moved closer, and she jumped when the heat of his lips set her neck aflame with soft, wet kisses.

"Landon, please let me go."

"You asking for my permission?" he rasped, trailing the tip of his tongue down her jaw until it skimmed along her lower lip.

"What are you—"

"Go ahead, Maggie. Let…go."

He accepted the open invitation of her mouth and swept inside, his tongue seeking hers, demanding she take part. More water fell from his hair, landing on her closed eyelids and cheeks, the coolness sizzling against her skin.

A low moan filled her chest and rumbled through her. Landon released her lips and buried his face against her neck. Then he freed her wrists and dug his fingers into her hair as he pressed his forehead to hers.

"Touch me, Maggie. Please touch me."

A shudder coursed through him as her hands slipped through the wet strands of his hair and brushed across his shoulders. His muscles flinched and tightened beneath her fingers, his flesh rising in goose bumps as she discovered the outline of his biceps and the undersides of his arms.

Maggie wasn't satisfied. She wanted to feel more—to feel all of him pressing hard against her. Arching against him, she trailed her hands down the side of his body, curving around his hips when suddenly he vanished from her touch. She landed hard against the door. It took a moment to open her eyes.

Landon stood three feet away with nothing but a white towel clenched low against his flat, hard stomach, partially covering a path of dark hair and the erection beneath.

"I can't do this," he punched out between breaths.

His free hand tightened into a fist at his side. His other squeezed the terry-cloth fabric, revealing more of the angled planes of his hipbones, accentuating the raw power of his body. His face was devoid of any emotion except regret.

"You're right, this shouldn't be happening."

Clawing at the door, Maggie yanked it open. She ran from the cabin, half-blind by tears, not waiting to hear the rest of his rejection.

"Isn't the tray a little light?"

Racy's voice rose above the deafening music of the Blue Creek house band. It was a typical Saturday night at the local roadhouse where Maggie's best friend had hired her as a waitress three months ago. Maggie hated the time away from Anna, but she needed all the extra money she could get. Today's horse sale notwithstanding.

Maggie leaned across the bar. "What did you say?"

Pointing at the empty bottles on the tray, Racy lifted replacements from the cooler. She popped the tops before setting them on the bar. "Call it the bartender in me, but I think a paying customer would rather have a full beer than an empty."

"Sorry." Maggie switched the bottles. "I guess my mind isn't here tonight."

"If I had a gorgeous hunk of cowboy waiting at home for me, do you think I'd be wasting time behind three feet of wood?"

"He isn't gorgeous, and he isn't waiting for me," Maggie shot back, surprised both her voice and hands remained steady.

"Oh, please. I ran into Anna and Nana B. last week at the ice-cream shop, and they sang his praises." Racy refilled the drinks for a couple of cowboys in front of her then turned her attention back to Maggie. "So, is he back from 'banging the barrier'?"

Maggie tucked a long strand of hair behind one ear. "If you're asking if he and Willie are finished working the fence line, the answer is yes."

Racy winked. "I like my way of putting it better."

"I know."

"According to your daughter and your grandmother, this guy is a walking, talking, card-carrying member of the Justice League."

"Anna barely knows Landon. She only met him for a few minutes. What did—" Maggie lowered her voice when the band switched to a country ballad. "What did they say?"

"More than you." With an air kiss, Racy thanked the cowboy who insisted she keep the hefty change from his tab, and tucked the money into her cleavage. "The guy is saving people left and right, making repairs with a single blow of his hammer, and to top it off—"

"No, there is no top." Maggie steadied her hand beneath the tray. "Landon Cartwright isn't a super hero. He isn't a saint. He is just another cowboy."

"Hmm, he certainly has blown your skirt up," Racy mused. "Since I haven't laid eyes on him yet, let me add if he can kiss as good as he does everything else, I'll move his rating from superhero to scrumptious demigod."

Maggie recalled Landon's mouth on hers and flushed, reliving the intensity of his kiss. Scrumptious? No, it far surpassed that and zoomed right into decadent.

She didn't know if he remembered kissing her—mouth gentle, touch hesitant—the night she'd brought him home. Nothing like this last time. The power in his hold pinning her hands to the door, the sureness of his lips on her neck. His mouth strong against hers. His desperate plea for her to touch him.

Right up until he backed away.

After racing from the cabin, she'd gone straight to her truck. Her family probably wondered why she hadn't said goodbye, but she couldn't face their inquisitive eyes. The sight of Landon in her rearview mirror, standing in the doorway in a pair of jeans and pulling a T-shirt over his head, stayed with her long after she'd gotten to the bar and hastily fixed her makeup.

Had he been coming after her? For what? To apologize?

Maggie didn't think she could take it. The regret in his dark eyes when he'd stared at her from across the cabin was clear enough.

Shaking off the memory, she lifted the tray.

Let it go, girl.

It was…hell, she didn't know what it was other than the best kiss of her life. The honest assessment made her arms shake like jelly. She struggled to balance the tray, and the bottles clanked together.

"Hey, you okay?"

Steadying herself, Maggie backed away before Racy could see her telltale blush. "I got it. I'm okay."

"You deliver those beers and get your butt back here." Racy easily twirled a bottle of whiskey on the palm of her hand before filling the glasses in front of her. "We need to talk."

"Last time I looked it was Max who signed my paycheck."

"He may be the owner, but I'm your boss." Racy tossed the bottle over one shoulder and caught it at hip level. "And that's an order."

Maggie stuck out her tongue and walked away. She made her way through the mob of thirsty revelers to one of her assigned tables. It didn't take long for the bottles to disappear and dollar bills to take their place.

Willie sat at a corner table with his regular group of cronies, all fellow senior-citizen cowboys. Maggie returned his wave and forced a smile. She'd purposely eavesdropped earlier when she'd heard him extolling Landon's hard work and list of ideas for the ranch.

I tell ya, boys, if Cartwright ain't once owned his own spread I'll eat my hat.

His words rang again in her ears. Had Landon once owned his own place? Maybe with his brother in Texas?

Maggie made her way back to the main bar. After cashing in, she found Racy at the far end.

"Jackie, take over," Racy called to the leggy brunette whose Daisy Duke cut-offs and lingerie-inspired corset made her a favorite among the cowboys. She then dragged Maggie to a shadowed back hallway. "Okay, girlfriend, spill it."

Maggie hugged her tray to her chest. Thankfully, the band was taking a break and the bar's sound system filled in with rowdy, but quieter, country rock. "Spill what?"

"Something's got your panties in a twist and I think it's your new hired hand. Weren't we talking a few weeks ago at the fair about you needing some fun? I think Cartwright might be the guy."

"Mess around with one of my employees? What about Anna? What kind of example would that set for her?"

"I'm not suggesting you do the wild thing in the middle of your living room. Come on, you know how to be discreet. And I know you're on birth control—"

Maggie pressed her hand over her friend's mouth, cutting off her words. "I'm on the Pill because it regulates me, not because of sex."

"Whatever. It's still not an issue." Racy leaned forward. "Maggie, this guy is temporary. He's gonna be gone once Hank's feeling fine and frisky again. Why not enjoy his company while he's—"

Racy's eyes flickered over Maggie's shoulder, her grin downright wicked. "Well, lookie here. I think you've already got someone checking you out."

"Who?"

Maggie started to turn, but Racy grabbed her. "Two o'clock, dressed in black from head to toe. My, that's a good-looking, tall drink of water."

Maggie frowned. "What are you talking about?"

"Well, isn't that what they always say about a handsome stranger in those westerns you love?" Racy smiled, then her eyes widened. "Ohmigod, is that him?"

Chapter Eight

Maggie spun around. Landon stood at the wall, apart from the crowded tables and swarming mass of people, his arms crossed over his chest and his booted feet crossed at the ankles. He was staring straight at her.

Oh, Lord, what was he doing here?

She didn't know what she'd say to him, but she'd hoped to have until tomorrow to think about it. She whirled back to Racy, her fingers gripping the tray.

"It *is* him!" Racy let loose a low wolf whistle. "Oh, yum. Take that cowboy, and the horse he rode in on, for a wild ride."

"Will you give it a rest?" Maggie groaned. "Not having sex isn't a crime, ya know."

"It is in my book. It's been so long for me, I consider it a class A felony."

"Then I'm your man."

Maggie gasped. For a moment, she thought the words might have come from Landon, but then she realized the deep, masculine voice came from over Racy's shoulder. She watched her friend's dark brown eyes widen. Shock filled her face, but it quickly disappeared with a toss of her flowing red hair as a tall man emerged from the shadows.

Maggie smiled at Destiny's sheriff. "Hi, Gage." His knowing grin told her he'd listened in on her and Racy. Had he heard everything? A wash of heat roared over her. "What brings you to the Blue Creek tonight?" she asked.

"Checking on things," he said as he tipped the brim of his Stetson. "How are you, Maggie?"

"Embarrassed to the tips of my toes, but otherwise I'm fine."

A teasing smile creased into deep dimples. "Don't worry, I didn't hear what you ladies were gossiping about." Then his grin disappeared. "How are things at the ranch?"

"Ah, good. Quiet, and have been for the last couple of weeks."

"I talked to Deputy Harris. You know we still aren't sure how Hank's wagon came apart. There's no evidence the wheel was tampered with, and Hank said he boned the spokes so they wouldn't chip."

"Which could result in the clean breaks when the wheel came off," Maggie said. "Leeann filled me in earlier today when we met at the station."

The sheriff nodded. "Kyle told me he'd fired Cartwright two weeks ago after his references didn't check out."

No, Kyle fired him after he rescued me.

Maggie forced herself not to look at Landon. "Really?"

"But I'm guessing his references checked out for you?"

Certain she could feel Landon's eyes boring into her back, Maggie shot a look at Racy, refusing to return her smirk. "Yes, everything is fine. Perhaps Greeley had another reason for letting Landon go."

"Could be." The sheriff nodded, then addressed Racy, his voice dropping to a low whisper. "Evening, Ms. Dillon."

Racy crossed her arms under her breasts, causing the ragged

neckline of her black tank top to reveal more of her ample cleavage and red satin bra. "Sheriff Steele."

Maggie had to give Gage credit. His eyes strayed only for a moment before he focused on her face. "Any chance of getting a cup of coffee?"

"We aim to please at the Blue Creek." Racy offered an arched brow as she brushed by the sheriff to step around the end of the bar. "Can I add a shot of something to improve your mood?"

"My mood is fine," Gage replied. "Any problems tonight?"

"Nothing I can't handle."

Gage frowned and took the mug. "Earlier this week—"

"By the time your boys appeared, I had the situation well in hand."

"I bet you did."

"Ah, Gage, I've been meaning to ask," Maggie cut in before Racy could respond. The fire flashing in her friend's eyes warned of another round of scathing comebacks—a favorite pastime of these two over the last fifteen years. "Nana B.'s birthday is next month. I hope you're free the last Saturday of August? You, too, Racy."

"Sorry, hon, no can do." Racy whisked away empty beer bottles and wiped at the wetness they left behind. "Got plans that weekend."

Gage took a swallow from the mug emblazoned with the Blue Creek logo before lowering it to the bar. "Me, too. I'll be out of town."

Racy wiped at the wetness the bottles left behind, her hand moving closer to where the sheriff's hand rested. So close, her electric-blue fingernails grazed his skin. Her friend was playing with Gage, and Maggie suspected the sheriff knew it.

"Oh?" Maggie persisted. "Where are you going?"

"Vegas."

Gage and Racy's eyes locked as they answered in unison.

"You're going to Vegas the last weekend of August?" Racy said.

Gage nodded. "For a law-enforcement forum."

"Great, the town will be overflowing with cops. I'm going for the Midwest regional in the All-American Bartending Challenge."

Maggie smiled. "Bartenders and cops? Sounds interesting. You think the town is big enough for the two of you?"

"I guess we'll find out." Gage took a step back and tapped the brim of his Stetson. "Maybe Ms. Dillon can get an Elvis look-alike to help with that *felony* problem of hers."

Racy's jaw dropped. She quickly regrouped and leaned over the bar. "Yeah, it'll take both of us to remove the stick you've got shoved up your—"

"Racy!" Maggie grabbed her friend's arm, and the sheriff walked away as if he hadn't heard. "Geez, the two of you never stop, do you?"

Racy pulled free. "Gage Steele is the most arrogant, condescending—"

Maggie cut her off with a grin. "Brave, sexy, honorable—"

"You think Gage is sexy?"

Maggie yanked hard on one of Racy's red curls. "Say it a little louder, why don't ya? Come on, you got to admit the man does great things to a pair of jeans."

"Oh, no, you aren't distracting me." Racy grabbed a beer and when one of the waitresses waved in their direction and pointed to her watch, she picked up the microphone. "Here, take a beer to your cowboy before I make you get your dancing boots on this bar."

She shoved the bottle at Maggie. "Go on, he won't bite. If I'm wrong, trust me, you'll love it."

Maggie's fingers tightened on the ice-cold bottle. She forced a deep breath, squared her shoulders and turned around.

Just another cowboy.

The words echoed in her head as she searched for Landon.

Racy's voice called out over the bar's sound system, her announcement bringing cheers from the crowd. Both sounded very far away.

Maggie made it through the maze of revelers to the back wall where Landon had stood.

He was gone.

The beer slid down too easy.

Sitting on the front porch of the foreman's cabin, Landon hooked his finger around the bottle's neck, balanced the bottom half on his knuckles and tipped his head back. Another long swallow of the cold liquid poured into his throat.

He hoped it would wash away the bitter taste he got remembering Maggie, standing with a cold one in her hand, looking for him.

He'd walked away from his spot against the wall when he recognized the man talking to Maggie and her redheaded friend as the sheriff. At the exit, he'd looked back. Confusion, and if he wasn't mistaken, hurt, flashed in her eyes when she'd scanned the crowd. Then her bartender friend had made an announcement he couldn't hear. He did see a group of Maggie's fellow waitresses climb on the bar as the band broke into old-time country rock.

When she'd walked away, he'd hightailed it out of there. Yeah, like he was going to stick around and watch those long legs of hers dance across the bar...

Dammit! Don't go there!

Hell, she'd probably gone back and told the local lawman to lock his ass up for laying that kiss on her earlier tonight. A kiss he could still feel.

Landon took another long gulp, mindful of his empty stomach and the two bottles he'd already finished. He'd hit the local market, bypassing the ready-made sandwiches for an ice-cold six-pack of America's finest, and headed home.

No, not home. This place isn't home no matter how relaxed you're feeling.

Landon grabbed the prepaid cell phone he'd picked up along with the beer and a pack of cigarettes. He punched in a familiar number and waited.

"Hel—Hello?" The greeting was hoarse and low.

Damn, Chase Cartwright sounded exactly like their father. A voice created from hard work and long hours spent outdoors. Landon's earliest childhood memory was his old man's voice. A voice silenced over ten years ago.

He washed away the memory with a long swallow of beer. "Hey, bro."

"Landon?"

"Yeah, it's me."

"Wh—what time is it?" A rustling filled the airwaves. "Damn, it's two in the morning. Is something wrong?"

Wrong? Yeah, I've got the hots bad for my boss. "Sorry, it's only going on one here. And does there have to be something wrong? Am I taking you away from someone?"

"If you were, I would've hung up on you by now." Chase yawned in Landon's ear and cleared his throat. "It's good to hear your voice, big brother."

Landon sighed, an ache in his chest. "Yours, too. It's been a while."

"Three months. How'd you end up in Wyoming?"

"How'd you know—oh, Storm told you." Landon realized the ranch's foreman must've filled him in. "It's a long story."

"Nothing with you is a long story," Chase said. "Tell me."

Using as few words as possible, Landon relayed his misadventures with G.W. and Maggie Stevens and how they led to the Crescent Moon.

"Boy, you never take the easy way." Chase chuckled. "This place doesn't sound like the others you've worked at."

"You don't know the half of it."

Landon dropped his hat to his side. He leaned against the porch railing, one boot on the top step, the other on the gravel path. With only moonlight to see by, he could easily spot a half-dozen needed chores. Not to mention the total rebuilding of the tool shed, his focus for tomorrow.

A warm breeze ruffled through the trees. It brought with it a feeling of comfort, a sense of home and family he hadn't felt in years, before his life was turned upside down. Nana B. and Anna were tucked safely in the house. Hank, too, who was sleeping in the study. Willie should be strolling in soon, and he guessed Maggie wouldn't be far behind.

They all belonged in this place. He was the outsider.

Another swig emptied the bottle. Landon realized he was missing much of what his brother was saying. Or maybe the beer was hitting him faster than he realized.

"And a lady boss, another first. Any easier to work for?" Chase continued. "I know how you like to take things over and run 'em your way."

"Storm tells me the ranch is doing well. You've done a great job taking care of the place, Chase."

A long pause filled the air. "Thanks, bro. It means a lot coming from you. I'm doing this for both of us."

Landon knew his brother wanted him home, but he couldn't go back. He never planned to set foot again on Still Waters. The ranch had caused him to lose the most precious thing in his life, leaving him with a shattered heart and burned soul.

He grabbed beer number four and wrenched off the top, the sharp edges of the cap tearing into his skin. "You approved the purchase of the horses?"

"Sure did. Storm was impressed with the information. It'll be a month or so before we can send someone to get them. No additional training needed?"

"They're superb. Maggie has a touch I've never seen before." Not counting Black Jack, who was being as obstinate as a creature could be.

"This Maggie sounds pretty special."

A long silence covered the miles between the two brothers.

"Look, I know Jenna carved you up pretty bad, long before you lost her and Sara," Chase said. "But you've got to stop blaming yourself for not being able to save them. You need to move on with your life. Find someone to heal—"

Landon gripped the phone so tightly he was sure it was going to shatter in his hand. "Don't go there, Chase. Not tonight. Please."

His brother must have heard something in his voice. "If that's what you want."

"I've got to go."

"Okay. Keep in touch."

Landon promised he would and ended the call. Special? Yes, Maggie was, but not for him. He didn't deserve anything special in his life.

Not anymore.

Landon tossed the phone on the porch floor and tilted the bottle to his mouth, draining half of it in seconds. He put it down and grabbed the pack of cigarettes. Placing one in his mouth, he dug into his pocket for matches.

His fingers found them and the smooth warmth of another object. Despite his silent command to leave it alone, his hand pulled out the silver locket. He stared at it, turning it repeatedly in his fingers.

Weeks had passed since he'd looked at Sara's picture, but he knew it by heart. Every curve of her sweet cheeks, the dark hair curled around her face and the trusting dark eyes, so much like his own. His baby girl. Taken from him only a few weeks after her second birthday.

He struck a match and opened the locket. The flame's glow danced over her features. Harsh, biting memories of a terrifying night crept out of the darkness. He closed his eyes against them and the sharp sting of tears.

"Don't burn yourself."

Landon's eyes flew open.

Maggie stood in front of him, her skin dark and smooth in the shadowed moonlight. She'd released her T-shirt from its tight knot, the hem loose at her waist. The short jean skirt made her legs appear long and lean. His gaze traveled the length of her, surprised when he saw her bare feet.

"Those things were killing me." She gestured at the pair of boots on the ground. "I didn't know you smoked."

"I don't." The cigarette bounced against his lips with his words. A raised eyebrow had him snatching the butt from his mouth. "I did, for a while…I quit."

"Yeah, I can see that," Maggie said. "When?"

He snapped the locket shut, curling it inside his fist, and dropped the match and the cigarette in an empty bottle. "About nine months ago. It's a nasty habit I picked up in—"

He clenched his jaw shut. *Way to go, genius.* Why not tell her the best way to survive the hellhole of prison was to have a cache of cigarettes because they were like gold?

Landon tucked the locket back into his jeans. The rest of beer number four disappeared as he looked out at the inky darkness of the nearby pond. "Ah, bad habits die hard, I guess."

He watched her from the corner of his eye. She nodded, but didn't reply. She didn't walk away either. Unable to stop himself, Landon looked at her. Was she waiting for him to offer to share the front stoop?

"What are you doing here?" he asked.

"I live here."

"I mean what are you doing *here?*"

She bit on her lower lip. "Do you mind if I join you?"

The effects of the alcohol fueled his curiosity. He waved at the porch. "It's your ranch."

She sat beside him. Dropping her purse to the ground next to her boots, she stretched her legs with a sigh. A sigh that could mean she was either glad to be off her feet or she wasn't looking forward to whatever she planned to say next.

Fisting her hands in her lap, she said, "We need to…ah, we need to talk."

Chapter Nine

The sight of her naked feet inches from the toe of his boot sent a stab of need through him. His body responded for the second time tonight.

No, make it the third.

"Landon?" Maggie's voice was soft. "Did you hear me?"

Talk. Yeah, she wanted to talk.

He braced himself. This was it. When he'd gotten back to the ranch, he'd waited to crack open the beer, sure the sheriff was on his way after Maggie told him how the hired help man handled her earlier. Then he figured it didn't matter if he was drunk or sober when the law came to haul his butt into town.

But time had passed. Now she was here. Alone.

She wasn't going to have him arrested. No, she was going to fire his ass.

But at least now he knew—the first kiss had been real. The ones they had shared on the other side of the wooden door behind them was all the proof he'd needed. He'd known the moment his mouth crashed down on hers.

"Yeah, I heard you." He looked at the bottle in his hand. Damn, these things were going too fast. He hoped she'd let him sleep it off before he had to hightail it off her land.

He returned the empty to the cardboard container and pulled out the last two. "Want one?"

Maggie hesitated. "I don't want to take your last one."

"This is my last one." He gestured with the bottle in his left hand. A smirk he couldn't stop pulled at the corner of his mouth. If he was out of here, he wasn't going to make it easy for her. Not when she'd wanted the kiss as much as he wanted it. "Come on, Ms. Stevens, aren't you in need of a little liquid courage?"

Annoyance flashed in her eyes. Good.

"Why not?"

She grabbed the bottle. Her fingers brushed across his and fire danced through his veins. He watched her pop the top, her lips cradling the opening as she tipped it. Eyelids fluttered closed, neck arched and breasts pushed out against the faded words on her T-shirt.

Down, boy.

Landon inhaled deeply, pulling in Maggie's magical scent of a summer's day and clean, fresh linen. Mixed with a trace of smoke from the bar and her sweat from a hard night's work. It intoxicated him.

When she lowered the bottle, a drop of liquid hung on her bottom lip. She brushed it away with the tip of her finger. "Mmm, tastes good. I'm usually the one handing beers to people, not the other way around…except for you. Where'd you go tonight?"

He busied himself opening his own beer. "I don't do well in crowds."

"How'd you know I worked at the Blue Creek, anyway?"

"Hank told me it was the best place to get a cold beer on a

Saturday night. I didn't know you'd be there until I saw you with your friends."

"Oh." Maggie took another sip. "Why didn't you join us instead of staring from across the room?"

"Like I said, you were with friends." Landon mirrored her movements with a long swallow. He wasn't about to tell her he avoided the law. "I don't mix business with pleasure."

A slight frown creased her brow. "Neither do I."

Here it comes. Landon swallowed hard and looked away. "Yeah?"

"Ah, I never—I need to thank you for the sale to your brother's ranch."

It took a second for him to process what she'd said. A thank-you before she kicked him to the curb? "I told you I didn't—"

"But you started the ball rolling," Maggie interrupted. "More than I've been able to do in the last few months. Thank goodness I got the offer to rehabilitate Black Jack."

"Willie said your work has been hit-or-miss with the beast."

"True, but it's part of the process. Just one more thing to do around here." Maggie's voice faltered before she continued. "That's what I need to talk to you about. I've got too much on my plate to…ah, to…well, to add anything else."

Relief flooded his veins. She wasn't firing him, she was warning him off.

He didn't understand the sudden desire to stay on this little scrap of land, but hell, at least he acknowledged it, if only to himself. It sat hard in the pit of his stomach. He didn't want to leave.

A sense of dizziness overwhelmed him. He closed his eyes and let his head drop back against the porch post. "Like what?"

"Excuse me?"

His eyes remained closed. "You said you've got a lot on your plate?"

"Well, there's Anna and the rest of my family."

"And Kyle Greeley."

"Yes, Kyle, too." She paused and he could feel her studying him. His skin prickled as if she'd touched him with her fingers instead of her gaze. "I suppose after you talked to Tommy, Willie told you about my dealings with Greeley."

Landon swallowed the bad taste her neighbor put in his mouth with another mouthful of beer. "Tommy?"

"Tommy Bailey, the sheriff's deputy."

Ah, right. Another reason for him to keep his distance. "Yeah, Willie loves to talk. His voice was the last sound I heard each night and the first I woke to each morning."

"What exactly did he tell you?"

Did the temperature drop a few degrees? Landon opened his eyes to find her staring out into the darkness. "He told me about your divorce and Greeley hanging around ever since. I guess that's why he's part of your crowded plate."

"Because the jerk has managed to steal away every cowboy I've hired in the last six months." Her voice had risen sharply before dropping again. "I'm not dating him."

A streak of protectiveness ran through him. His fingers tightened on the beer bottle. "Who said anything about dating? I was talking about your land, your horses—"

"Yes, he's after both, but he's not getting either. How could I put a price on this place? My family has been here over a hundred years. It's a part of me, a part of my history. If I didn't have the Moon I don't know where I would go, what I'd do."

The powerful love in her voice caused a band to tighten around Landon's chest. How easy would it have been for her to sell out? To start over away from the one place that must carry a heavy load of pain and heartache thanks to the way her father treated her?

Like you did?

He'd made the choice to walk away from Still Waters years ago. And he hadn't missed it. Not once. But when he tried to imagine what it would be like to know his family's ranch wasn't there, wasn't a part of him, he couldn't.

"I don't think Kyle understands," she continued, her voice softer. "He doesn't have the same connection to his land."

"Why?"

"Richard Greeley, the original owner of the Triple G, was a bachelor, but I guess he was quite a busy man in his youth. Rumor has it he's got a few kids scattered around the country. Kyle showed up about eight years ago when Richard got sick. It took a blood test before the old man would accept him as his son. When he died, Kyle took over."

"So why is he interested in this land?"

"I don't know. Greeley's sunk a lot of money into his own place and into the town, which is good for Destiny, but it inflated his already oversized ego. It's like he's trying to buy his way in."

"Including the sheriff's office?"

"No." Maggie's denial was absolute. "I've known Gage— Sheriff Steele—since we were kids. He's one of the good guys."

Landon wasn't so sure, considering the way Steele's deputy gushed about Kyle, but he kept his opinion to himself.

"Anyway, old man Greeley died five years ago, around the same time as my father. When my husband walked out, Kyle started sniffing around. Romance didn't work, so now he's trying to use the local bank—"

She broke off her tirade and tipped the bottle to her lips. She finished her mouthful of beer with a swipe of pink tongue. He watched, unable to pull his gaze from her mouth.

He forced himself to look away. "Do you think Greeley's behind all the problems you've been having?"

"There's no proof, despite Willie's ramblings. Maybe its bad karma…I don't know, but I can't work on what-ifs, I have to go with what I do know. And I know I can't take any chances right now. I can't get distracted." Maggie's words rushed out of her mouth. "What happened between us tonight wasn't anyone's fault, but it can't happen again. I need you, at least until Hank is back on his feet. You must see me as some desperate-divorcée-slash-lonely-single-mother out for a quick roll in the sack, but I'm not. I'm—"

"Okay."

She blinked. "Okay?"

Did he read hesitancy in her gaze? Her speech came out rehearsed, as if she'd repeated it all the way home. Was she second-guessing herself now?

It didn't matter. She was right.

He guessed he should thank her for reminding him he was still a man with a man's desires. Nevertheless, the two of them were as different as people could be. No, he had to stay away from Maggie for reasons much deeper. Giving into his craving would only end in heartache for her because that's all he had to give. Passion, desire, lust. He could describe it half a dozen ways, but none had the word *forever* attached to it.

And Maggie was a forever kind of woman.

Too bad his body wasn't listening. Landon grabbed his hat and jammed it on. It took what was left of his strength—and he was about empty—to look her straight in the eye. "I said okay. As in, 'You're right. It'll never happen again.'"

"Yes." Her breath rushed out with the word. "Never again."

An overwhelming urge to blow her words to hell with one kiss rose from deep inside. He ignored it and stood. A white-hot ripple of pain shot across his back. He grabbed the porch railing. *Dammit, not now!*

Maggie jumped to her feet. "Are you all right?"

No, I'm horny, hurting and halfway to hell.

"I'm fine. I'm going to bed." He placed a foot on the bottom step. The pain exploded, and his knees buckled.

"Whoa, not on your own, you're not." Maggie caught him with her body and wrapped her arm around his waist. She grabbed his hand and held it when his arm landed across her shoulders. "Thought it would take more than a few beers to topple you."

Landon let her believe it was the alcohol incapacitating him as they hobbled to the front door. Her scent filled his head and her body heat branded him from his chest to his knees. He didn't think it was possible, but his erection pulled his boxer briefs tighter. The only light in the room came from a small bedside lamp. When they got to the quilt-covered brass bed, he let go and sat on the edge.

"Wait here a minute," she said.

As if his body would allow him to go anywhere. Landon dropped his hat to his lap, his eyes glued to her backside. She faded into the dark shadows of the kitchen. He heard water running and a cabinet door open and close.

"Here, this will help." She started back toward him, holding out a glass of water. "Drink all of it. You'll be thankful in the morning."

After doing what he was told and handing her the empty glass, he leaned back and braced himself with locked arms. He had to lie down, the sooner the better, but his damn boots had to come off first. He tried to toe one off while Maggie refilled the glass and put it on the table.

"Thanks," he muttered. He agreed with what she'd said on the porch. Anything between them would be one hundred percent wrong, but it was killing him to have this woman and a soft bed so close together. "I've got it from here."

"Sure you do."

Before he could protest, she dropped to her knees in front of him. The air was sucked from the room and his chest. His fingers fisted into the aged quilt beneath him as he looked at the top of her blond head.

"Real cowboys don't sleep with their boots on." She pulled

each boot free and set them on the floor. Standing, she grabbed his hat off his lap. "Or their hats."

His breathing returned to normal when she rose, but the brush of his Stetson across the front of his jeans had him scooting backwards. Ignoring the pain, both the good and the bad, he lay flat and yanked the quilt over his midsection. "You'd better go before we both forget the speech you made, boss lady."

He saw her hand freeze for a moment as she reached for the light. One click and the room dropped into darkness, leaving the moonlight streaming through the windows and open doorway.

She stepped onto the porch. "Are you going to be okay?"

No, but he was used to not being okay. He closed his eyes. "Maggie, go."

Burning heat. It surrounded him, clung to his skin like a layer of plastic he dragged with every step. It coated his eyes, his tears doing little to assist in his desperate need to see what lay in front of him.

He fell to the floor, stretched out his hands and pulled himself along. It felt like hours, his voice raw from calling out, his ears straining to hear the slightest sound that would tell him which direction to turn.

All around him were the cries of dying wood. His rational side screamed at him to leave this place. His irrational side forced him forward, muscles twisting in agony. Without warning, he found what he'd been searching for. It singed his fingers, but he refused to let go.

Dragging himself inch by inch, he retreated from the heat, refusing to give in to the exhaustion, moving toward the blessed fresh air. At last, he gulped in life-giving breaths.

He heard whispers, but didn't understand them. There was no time to reason, to think, he must keep moving. Then a scream roared from deep inside and the hand of the devil captured his soul and dragged him back to the fire—

Landon vaulted upright in the large brass bed, a silent scream on his lips. His wide, unseeing eyes blinked rapidly. His fingers clenched at the sweat-soaked sheets. Forcing himself to breathe deeply, he began to recognize his surroundings. It was only a nightmare. A nightmare he'd thought was out of his head. Out of his heart. A shuddering breath filled him. It'd lasted longer tonight than ever before. This time he'd heard the whispers, but couldn't make out the words.

What was she trying to tell him?

He raised his hands to cover his face. Sleep wouldn't come again. Hell, he didn't want it to. He shoved back the blankets and sat on the edge of the bed. At least the pain in his back was gone. Too bad he couldn't say the same about his head. A shower helped, and the aspirin he took would kick in soon. Thankful for no signs of life from the main house despite the sky beginning to lighten with the coming dawn, he stepped outside and found the cell phone sitting on the porch railing.

He wished he could say he didn't know why the nightmare was back, but he did. A thought had come to him before he fell asleep. And it meant another phone call home. He hesitated calling this early but he knew his friend's private line went to his office. He could always leave a message, but he had a feeling Bryce would be awake.

"Powers." A strong voice answered immediately.

"Hey, Buckshot."

"Well, I'll be damned," the low voice said, then chuckled. "It's the Cartwright Kid."

Landon wanted to grin at the familiar use of their childhood nicknames, but the heaviness in his heart wouldn't allow it. "How you doing, Bryce?"

"Same as always. Living large, loving life, thanks to the

triplets up at this godawful hour. Geez, it's been forever since we talked. Don't tell me you're home?"

"No, I'm not."

A long pause filled the air. "Okay, at least tell me you've talked to your brother recently. We're meeting for lunch later today."

Landon went on alert. "We talked last night. Is something wrong?"

"No, strictly a social thing. MaryAnn wants to show off the girls and try to fix up your brother with one of her friends. Now, you want to tell me why you're calling at the butt-crack of dawn? Is it dawn where you are?"

Landon watched as the sun broke over the horizon. "Yeah, it is. I'm sorry I called so early. I don't have any right to ask, but I need your help."

"Hey, no time or distance—"

"Or evil varmint or wanton saloon girl can come between the Daredevil Duo." Landon's words joined Bryce's as they recited their childhood oath together. The reminder of their lifelong friendship had him blinking away a sudden stinging in his eyes. He quickly blamed the bright sunrise.

Bryce Powers, one of the winningest lawyers in the state of Texas, had refused to give up on him after he was found guilty. He'd worked tirelessly to prove the fire that took Sara and Jenna wasn't an act of arson, but a horrific accident, resulting in Landon getting his freedom back.

A freedom he couldn't convince himself he deserved.

"So, what's up?" Bryce asked.

Landon told him about Maggie, the ranch and Kyle Greeley. "It's probably nothing, but I need to know how much of a threat Greeley is to the Crescent Moon—see if anything strikes you the wrong way. If you could keep this as quiet as possible, I'd appreciate it."

"How do I get a hold of you if I find anything?"

Landon gave him the cell phone number and said goodbye. He headed for the barn, questioning why he'd made the call. Because Maggie didn't fire his ass when she had every right to? Or because he didn't want to see another woman and her little girl hurt on his watch?

Black Jack stood quietly at the open doorway of his stall, which connected to the large corral. The moment Landon moved from under the trees, the wild mustang raced outside.

"Are you coming to say good morning?" He moved to the edge of the corral. "Or warn me off?"

Black Jack galloped back and forth behind the fence. The closer Landon got the more agitated the horse became. He stopped, giving the mustang a chance to catch his scent. "See, boy, I'm not out to hurt you. No one here is."

The horse reared and shook his head as if he didn't believe him.

"Yeah, I know. But you've got a good thing here if you're smart enough to realize it. A nice place to sleep, plenty of grub and if you'd get over yourself, there's a couple of pretty fillies inside who'd like to get to know you."

Black Jack offered a loud snort in reply and backed away.

"Who am I to be giving advice?" Landon mumbled as he made his way into the barn. He checked on G.W., the words he'd said to Black Jack ringing in his head. Hell, was he talking about the animal or himself?

Refusing to allow his mind to go down that road, he let G.W. and the rest of the horses free in the paddock on the other side of the barn, glad to see his friend fully healed.

As he mucked out the stalls, the whispered words from his nightmare returned.

It was Jenna. She was trying to tell him something with her dying breath. He could hear the husky tone of her voice, but couldn't make it all out. More likely, he didn't want to understand what she was saying.

Your…fault…Sara…not…me…

He gripped the rack, the veins in his hands pushing tight against his skin.

"Stop," he whispered between clenched teeth. "I know it's my fault. I know I didn't…I couldn't…"

With a pile of dirty hay covering his boots, he gave in and yanked the locket out of his pocket. Opening it, he looked at the words engraved opposite the picture.

To My Daddy, Love Sara.

Jenna had given it to him on their six-month anniversary, the night their daughter was born. Back then he'd thought their shotgun marriage might work. Too bad he'd found his wife in bed with one of his ranch hands six months later. He didn't let on he'd seen them, but she knew. The fact he'd moved into another bedroom and sent the cowboy packing had been enough of a clue. He'd spent the better part of the next year as far away from Jenna and Sara as he could. Until he'd realized he was punishing his daughter for something she'd had no part of. He'd vowed on her second birthday to be the kind of father she needed.

A vow made too late.

"Good morning."

Landon spun around. The locket fell from his hands into the pile of straw, dirt and manure at his feet. "Sh—ah, hell, what are you doing here?"

A pair of green eyes widened. "You're lucky my mama didn't hear you." Tiny fists jammed into her overalls. "Do you know how yucky a bar of soap tastes? Besides, I live here."

Like mother, like daughter. Other than the first day when this pint-sized version of Maggie had flung her arms around him in a surprise hug, Landon hadn't seen Anna Stevens, thanks to spending the last two weeks camping out with Willie. Oh, he knew all about her. Willie's ramblings made sure of that. He didn't talk about Maggie without talking about her little girl.

And how Alan Stevens had walked out on the two of them.

Landon had gone to sleep many nights wondering how a man did such a thing. Lord knows, his marriage to Jenna was over long before her death, but he never would've walked out on his daughter. Had Sara lived, she'd be a few years younger than the girl in front of him.

Tears burned at the edges of his eyes. He looked away. "Ah, sorry. You surprised me."

Landon turned his back to her, blinked away the stinging and stared at the ground. The locket was gone. He bent down and started to search.

"Whatcha looking for?"

He froze at the sound of Anna's voice. Closing his eyes, he willed the little girl to go away. "Nothing. Something I dropped."

"Can I help?" She plunked down beside him and started tunneling through the hay. "Mama always says four eyes are better than two when you've lost something."

Her hair, blonder than her mother's, hung loose over her shoulders. A deep breath drew in the mixture of baby powder and stale hay. Tightness seized his chest. When she turned and peeked at him through her hair, his heart told him to look away. He couldn't.

"Ya know?" She offered a grin with two missing teeth. "I'd be a whole lot better at this if I knew what I was looking for."

Forcing his gaze from her, Landon focused on pushing around the hay and dirt. "Ah, you should go back to the house."

"Why?"

"Because your mom might be looking for you."

"Why would she—oh, I found it." Anna jumped up, the open locket cradled in her palm. "Is this what you're looking for? Wow, what a pretty baby. Is she yours? What's her name?"

Landon jerked to his feet. He took the locket and shoved it back into his pocket. A throat cleared behind him softly. His body turned to stone.

"Mama!"

Anna raced across the barn and Landon forced himself to

face Maggie, who squatted to return her daughter's hug. His throat closed, choking off his breath.

"Are you bothering Mr. Cartwright?" Maggie asked, voice low as she smoothed her daughter's hair.

"Nope." Anna squirmed away. She offered him a bright smile. "Am I?"

He could do nothing but shake his head.

Maggie rose to her feet, eyes still on her daughter. "Well, you better get back inside, young lady. Since you insisted on being up so early, you can help Nana B. get breakfast on the table."

The little girl pouted, but after a gentle swat on her backside, she left the barn. Maggie followed, not once looking Landon in the eye.

Chapter Ten

"No, I didn't ask him yet."

"One reason." Racy's voice rang loud through the phone above the noisy din of the Sunday afternoon crowd at the Blue Creek Saloon. "Give me one damn reason why you haven't asked Landon about his daughter. And it better be good."

"I've been busy." Maggie tucked the cordless phone between her ear and shoulder and reached for another pillowcase to fold. A week had gone by since she'd come across Anna and Landon in the barn in time to hear—she wasn't sure exactly what. "Besides, I'm not clear on what he said."

"Bull. You're scared."

"Language!"

"Stop mothering me and ask the man."

"It's been crazy around here. I have a ranch to run—"

Racy cut her off by clucking like a chicken.

Maggie didn't respond. From her window, she could see Landon on his hands and knees, finishing the repairs to the deck next to the pond. Jeans, faded in all the right places, showed off his backside and muscular thighs to perfection. The plain white T-shirt pulled tight across his back emphasized the width of his shoulders and darkness of his skin. His black cowboy hat covered his hair except for the ponytail lying between his shoulder blades.

"Hello? Girlfriend? Did I lose you?"

"I'm here."

Her gaze moved to Anna, who stood nearby with Mr. Darcy, her oversized orange tabby, in her arms. Anna said something and Landon paused, resting back on his heels as he responded. He stroked the cat's fur then directed Anna to step back when Mr. Darcy began to squirm. Anna willingly complied.

Maggie smiled.

Her daughter had become Landon's shadow from the moment he'd given her a ride on G.W., allowing her to circle the corral a few times after he'd quizzed her about her riding experience. She'd followed him everywhere since then, peppering him with questions and little-girl chatter. At first, Landon had looked shaken and avoided her whenever possible. Two days later, he'd waved off Maggie's latest apology for her daughter's persistence and appeared resigned to Anna's presence. Now, it looked like he actually enjoyed it.

"You're certainly quiet," Racy chimed in. "Let me guess. Mr. Tall, Dark and Positively Yummy is providing a distraction?"

"Racy…"

"Oh, please, like you haven't enjoyed working with him, and the man does like to work. Hell, other than to say hello, he didn't look twice at me when I was there for dinner the other night."

"Lord knows, that rarely happens." Maggie tried to ignore the thrill shooting through her at Landon's immunity to her best friend's considerable charms.

"Ha-ha. His eyes certainly followed your every move."

"So you keep telling me, but except for meals, we've rarely seen each other. Hank is feeling better now, leaving me free to concentrate on the horses, especially Black Jack." Maggie's gaze flittered toward the black mustang in his corral. "He's accepting the saddle and I spent some time riding him yesterday. I'd never be this far along if Landon didn't start work long before sunup. It's like he's driven to get this place in tip-top shape."

Racy snorted. "Something you're not used to seeing in a man under age fifty."

Yes, but it was something else, too. She hadn't confided in Racy about the passionate kiss they'd shared last week, or about when she'd made it clear she wanted nothing from him but an honest day's work. He was sticking to their agreement and staying as far away from her as his job allowed.

But he did watch her. She could feel his eyes on her all the time, and to be fair, she spent a good part of each day watching him, too. And the nights. Oh, she couldn't think about her wild dreams without blushing all the way to the tips of her toes.

"Imagine what he could do if he put those muscles to work on you," Racy continued. "Say, in the hayloft or by the creek? Oh, I know—how about the porcelain tub your great-great-grand-whatever dragged out West decades ago."

"Racina Josephine!"

Landon glanced over his shoulder, and despite the sun reflecting off the window Maggie swore she could feel the heat of his gaze. She spun away, clutching the pillowcase she was folding to her breasts, the pang of squashed desire so strong it ached.

Racy laughed. "Okay, I'll stop. So, how come I had to hear about your horse sale at the bar instead of from you?"

The air rushed from Maggie's lungs. "Who told you?"

"What? Is it a secret?"

"No, not exactly."

She'd wanted to keep the sale under Kyle Greeley's radar as long as she could. Of course, he probably had ways of finding out about the sizable increase in her bank account. Along with the fee for training Black Jack, the sale would put a nice dent in the final loan payment due the end of next month. She was already trying to secure another loan from a bank in Cheyenne to pay off the remainder.

"Like I said, I've had a lot on my mind lately."

"Sexy cowboys notwithstanding. So, are you coming into work early to help me with this crowd?"

"I shouldn't. It'd serve you right to be stuck alone with all those thirsty, NASCAR-loving cowboys. Do you think Leeann will stop by?"

"Doubtful. I told her Bobby had the pole position and everyone was gathering to cheer on the hometown hero. You would've thought I was talking about the weather for all the reaction I got, but what else is new."

Maggie had also noticed the difference in Leeann since she'd come back to town. Long gone was the vivacious girl they'd known, who'd always persevered despite an overprotective father and beauty-pageant-obsessed mother. "I'm not surprised. We had lunch together last week and she was—I don't know. I can't describe it, but she sure has changed from the girl she was twelve years ago."

"We all have—" Racy's voice dropped away. "Hey, cowboy! You touch that bottle of tequila, and I'll chop off the protruding parts of your body and serve them to you on toast."

Maggie grinned. "Not all of us have. You're the same sweet, loving girl you've always been."

"Damn straight," Racy said. "And you better bring some 4-1-1 with you when you come in later, or I'm gonna corner that cowboy myself. I know I'm not the only one with questions."

Maggie ended the call. Racy was right. She did have questions for Landon, but in light of her "I'm the employer, you're the employee" speech, she didn't feel right asking about his personal life.

This is what you wanted. Space and separation. You made it clear. He's being paid to do a job, not romance you.

And what a job he'd done. The tool shed, rebuilt from the ground up, stood strong with a fresh coat of red paint. Both the bunkhouse and the foreman's cabin sported new, dark-brown paint. A second, smaller barn was almost finished in the same color, and the main house was next on the list. Gallons of bright-white paint waited in the cool shade of the porch.

Together with Willie and Hank, he'd completely reorganized the inside of the main barn, including the addition of a new watering system for each of the stalls. She didn't think she could afford it until Willie showed her Landon's cost-effective plans.

"What would I do without—" Maggie bit hard at her bottom lip, stopping her words. She blinked, refusing to acknowledge the freshly folded clothes on her bed appeared watery and out of focus.

She couldn't do this.

So what if everyone treated him like he was family?

Nana B. had gone out of her way to make apple cobbler after she'd discovered he loved it. Hank and Willie easily followed his lead on the never-ending list of ranch chores. Her daughter had a serious case of hero worship, and if Maggie let herself, she could easily fall in—

The slam of the screen door made her jump. Her heart thumped in her chest, and she brushed away the moisture on her eyelashes. Scuffling noises told her someone was searching for something.

She headed to the kitchen. "What are you looking for, munchkin?"

Anna opened and rummaged through cabinet drawers in quick succession. "Nothing."

"What does this nothing look like?"

"Mama, please. I'm in a hurry."

Maggie smiled and leaned against the counter. "I've got to go into work early tonight. I know we planned to christen the new deck when Hank and Willie got back, but we'll wait until tomorrow, okay?"

"Sure, mama, whatever." Anna slammed the last drawer shut and raced out of the kitchen, her blond braids bouncing against her shoulders.

"Honey, what are you—" Maggie stopped when Anna came back in with a pair of scissors in her hand. "Anna?"

"I'm walking, Mama," she said, moving slowly toward the back door and holding the shears correctly. "I'm walking."

"Walking where?"

"To Landon's." Her voice carried through the screen door when it shut behind her. "I'm gonna give him a haircut."

It took a moment for the words to register. When they did, Maggie bolted after her daughter. Anna had quickened her pace and was at the cabin's steps by the time Maggie caught her.

"Hold on a minute, honey." She latched onto her daughter's arm. "What do you mean by 'haircut'?"

"Landon says his hair is getting in his way and he's going to the barber's," Anna explained, wiggling from Maggie's fingers. "I told him I could cut it, and he said okay."

For a moment, the woman in her mourned the loss of her cowboy's thick, black hair. The first time she'd seen it, loose and flowing, it had touched off a yearning so deep she immediately attributed it to the teenage rebellious side she'd thought long dead.

Her more mature adult side had Maggie reprimanding her child. "Anna, what have I told you about telling fibs—"

"Honest, Mama." Anna's eyes widened. "He said I could."

"You must have misunderstood—"

"She didn't." Landon stood in the doorway of the cabin with a towel over one shoulder, a wooden chair in one hand and a stack of newspapers in the other. "You ready, Miss Anna?"

Anna walked up the steps. "Yup!"

Maggie was right behind her. "Landon, you can't be serious. She's—"

"Going to cut my hair," he interrupted, his full attention on Anna as he set the chair in the middle of the porch. "Here, I'll hold those scissors while you put the newspapers down so we don't make a mess."

"Okay." Anna grinned, and laid the newspaper around the chair. "How much should I use?"

"It's not like you're shaving a polar bear. I'm just a man."

A man who'd paid more attention to her little girl in the last week than Anna's father had in the last two years.

Anna giggled. Maggie smiled as she crossed her arms over her chest.

"You sure about this?"

He looked at her. A heart-tugging tenderness filled his eyes. She'd seen that emotion before. Long ago in Alan's eyes when Anna was first born. Was Landon thinking of his own—

"It's hair, Maggie." He paused, as if he was going to say something more, but he pressed his lips closed. The pained emotion in his gaze disappeared. "It'll grow back. Besides, she's only cutting off the pony tail."

Unable to trust her voice, she nodded. They were alone for the first time in a week, as alone as one could be with an eight-year-old chaperone, but Maggie's heart raced all the same.

He turned and spoke directly to Anna. "All set?"

"All set." Anna took the scissors he held out to her. "My mom cuts mine, Hank's and Willie's hair all the time. I know what I'm doing. Have a seat."

Landon sat and arranged the towel so it lay flat over his shoulders. He shook out his hair, then gathered it at his neck with a piece of rawhide. "Cut above the string, okay?"

"Gotcha."

Anna went to work. Maggie sidled past Landon, a shimmer

of electricity grazing her skin where their arms brushed. "I'll watch from back here."

"I'm doing fine, Mama," Anna said, her tongue tucked into the corner of her mouth. "I'm—oops!"

A chunk of black hair and two pieces of rawhide dropped to the newspaper.

"Oops?"

Landon's voice sounded calm, but the muscles across his shoulders tightened.

Maggie stared at her daughter's handiwork and hid a smile behind her fingers. Anna looked at her with wide, pleading eyes. "You better answer your customer, young lady."

"I, ah…I cut below the knot."

"So it stayed right where I put it," Landon said. "Do you want to try again?"

"What in tarnation are you three up to?"

Maggie whirled at the sound of Willie's voice. He and Hank were heading for the cabin, a large cardboard box in Willie's arms quivering on its own.

"I'm giving Landon a haircut," Anna said proudly. "Who's next?"

"I think I'm all set, Little Bit," Hank replied.

"Me, too," Willie said, "but we've got somep'n—ah, a few somep'ns for ya."

"Me?" Anna handed the scissors to Maggie and scrambled down the steps. Willie dropped to one knee and put the box on the grass.

"What's going on?" Maggie asked. "How'd your appointment with Doc go?"

"Ah, fine. It went fine." Hank cradled his ribs with one hand. "But I've got to wear these blasted bandages for a while longer. Ain't that right, Willie?"

"Ah, yeah," Willie piped up. "Maybe another week."

"Or two," Hank quickly added.

"Or three. Looks like we need you around here a bit longer, Cartwright."

Hank nudged Willie with the toe of his boot, an action not lost on Maggie. She glanced at Landon, and followed his gaze to Anna and the writhing box she was helping Willie open. "What's in—"

"Kittens!" Anna's gleeful cry filled the air along with cries and meows from tiny balls of fluff. "Wow, look at them!"

Maggie groaned inwardly as her daughter fell into the box. "William Howard Taft Perkins." She eyed the cowboy who managed to look chagrined and prideful at the same time. "Are you out of your mind?"

Hank backed away with a wry smile on his face. "I better take a few of those pain pills before I head to my place. Doctor's orders."

Doctor's orders, my ass. Hank knew when to hightail it to safety. Maggie crossed her arms and stared balefully at her other cowboy.

"Now, you know Ms. Kali's office is right next to the doc's office." Willie tried to keep the squirming kittens inside. "Her assistant found the kittens by the side of the road. They're all healthy, and she was taking them to a shelter in Cheyenne. No telling where they'd end up."

"Oh, they are so cute." Anna picked up two of the kittens, one white and the other black. She buried her cheeks in their fur.

Maggie knew she was in trouble.

"Here, hold one." Anna offered the black kitten to Landon who caught it just before it wiggled off his lap. He let out a sound Maggie could've sworn was laughter as he held the kitten close to his chest.

"Hey there, little one." He easily cupped the animal in one large hand, its tiny claws sinking into the towel as it nuzzled his neck. "Where are you going?"

"Not sure how your Mr. Darcy is going to feel about these intruders," Landon said to Anna as he stroked the kitten's back.

"Mr. Darcy can be their mamma."

Maggie choked back her own laughter.

Landon's eyebrows rose. "Ah, I thought Mr. Darcy was a boy cat."

Anna tipped her head to one side. "So?"

Landon shot a questioning glance at Maggie. "You want to handle this?"

"Oh, no, you're doing fine," she said, then grinned.

"I think I'll show Mr. Darcy his new babies." Anna put the kittens back into the box. "Can you carry them for me, Willie?"

"Whatever you say, little lady."

Willie scrambled to his feet and made a hasty retreat with Anna on his heels. Maggie watched them go. Her head told her she needed to make a few phone calls to find good homes for the kittens. Her heart? That was something different. She doubted Mr. Darcy would have any interest in the miniature versions of himself, but Anna was a nurturer, like her.

"I think I've been abandoned." Landon crossed his arms over his chest, pulling the T-shirt snug against his muscular arms. "Guess I've got nothing compared to a couple of balls of fluff."

Oh, I wouldn't say that. Maggie forced her gaze to stay on his face and away from those tanned, rippling muscles. "Sorry. You know the attention span of little girls."

His jaw hardened and his gaze flattened. "No, actually I don't." He dropped his arms and started to rise. "I plan to restock the tool shed this afternoon. I'll get to it after I head into town—"

"Stay put." Maggie pushed his shoulder and at first he resisted, his body hard and unmoving. Then he dropped back into the chair. She yanked her hand away, willing herself not to rub it against her jeans in an attempt to erase the tingling sensation. "I'll finish your haircut."

"You don't have to—"

"I want to, I mean, it's the least I can do after your bravery at letting Anna give it a try. Do you mind—" She motioned to the open cabin door.

"It's your ranch."

"Be right back."

Maggie went inside, heading for the bathroom. She tried to ignore the rumpled bed sheets and Landon's personal care items on the sink.

His closed expression at her comment about little girls had her wondering again about his daughter. How old was she? Where did she live? Had Landon been married? Not that that was a requirement to have a child nowadays. Did she dare ask him about this?

"Maybe you should mind your own business," Maggie muttered, a packet of new combs in the cabinet catching her eye. *Ah, success.* Heading back to the front porch, she half expected to see the taillights of Landon's truck pulling out of the drive, but he sat still in the chair.

She moved behind him and pulled the remains of the rawhide from his hair. His shoulders stiffened again and she couldn't stop herself from pressing her knuckles gently into his rigid muscles. "Relax, I'm good at this."

He didn't reply, but his upper body did soften a bit, if it was possible for solid muscle to do so. Maggie pulled the comb through his shorn locks. A giggle escaped her as she surveyed the ragged edges falling below the neckline of his shirt.

"That bad, huh?"

"Nothing I can't fix. How short do you want it?"

"Whatever, I trust you."

His words made her pause.

Don't be silly, it's a haircut. Don't make anything more of it.

She started cutting, his hair sliding through her fingers like smooth silk. The heat of the day lifted his natural scent—one part hay, one part hard work—and it enveloped her. She brushed the back of his neck and he hummed softly.

"You've got a soft touch, Maggie."

She clenched hard on the comb and scissors at the rumble of his voice.

Concentrate, girl, concentrate.

Chapter Eleven

The air was heavy with the sudden quiet. Landon shifted in his seat, his shoulders taut as he crossed his arms over his chest. "I found your ranch shirt in my latest batch of laundry. Don't let me forget to give it back to you."

Anger and pain Maggie had thought long gone rushed through her, erasing any thought of Anna. "I don't want it. Keep it, toss it, I really don't care."

"This from the ranch's owner?"

"I'm sure Willie shared with you the history of the Moon and my less-than-stellar relationship with my father. Those shirts were his toys, prizes he gave out to his favorites."

"But not to you."

"On my sixteenth birthday I found one of those shirts in the bathroom and I foolishly thought my father had left it there as a gift," she said, as she dropped her hands to his shoulders, angling the scissors into a safe position. "I didn't have it on ten minutes before he hauled me into his office and told me no woman would ever wear one of his shirts. I never did. I thought I got rid of them all after he died."

She took a deep breath and trimmed his hair, catching sight of Hank and Willie as they drove away in Hank's truck. She didn't know what she would've done growing up if not for those two stand-in daddies. They'd bandaged more cuts, dried more tears and showered her with way more love and affection than she'd ever received from her real father.

"I was four when my mother ran off with one of my daddy's cowboys," she continued, the words rolling off her tongue like a conveyer belt. "It took a while to figure out I was a constant reminder of my mother's betrayal."

Her words hung in the air for a moment before Landon spoke. "I take it Nana B. wasn't here then?"

Maggie pulled in a breath and remembered the day she'd found the petite, white-haired woman on her front porch. "No, she didn't come to the Crescent Moon until I was a newlywed. Nana B. is my mother's mom, and she'd lost contact with her daughter years before. She found us thanks to a private detective."

"Your dad was okay with her?"

"He welcomed her once he got a taste of her cooking. I'm better with horses than I am in the kitchen." Finished with the back and sides, Maggie moved to stand in front of him. She didn't want to think about how her father had mellowed after she and Alan had married. Of course, Alan was the son he'd always wanted. "Ah, can you tip your head to the left a bit?"

Landon shuffled his feet, making room for her between his thighs and tilted his head. "Like this?"

She placed her fingertips on his chin. "A bit more…"

His gaze latched onto hers, and she was powerless to look away. Coal-black eyes framed by equally dark lashes roamed her face before pausing on her mouth. Then he looked back into her eyes.

"Being a single parent isn't easy."

Maggie flushed and straightened. She could only imagine what Willie had said about Alan, considering the old man had never seen her ex-husband as anything but, to use his own words, a flannel-mouthed blowhard.

Since Alan had left, his contact with Anna had dwindled. During their early marriage, he'd been a fun-loving, attentive dad. But now Anna and she were on their own.

"I'm not raising Anna by myself." Maggie returned to cutting his hair. "I've got Nana B. and my extended family and friends."

"You're a great mom, Maggie."

His soft words sank into her soul and tears sprang to her eyes. She was embarrassed at how much his simple words meant to her. Even with her family to help, Maggie thought, Anna was her responsibility. And her joy and proudest achievement.

Taking a step back, she couldn't help looking at Landon's face. A sigh of relief bubbled in her throat. His eyes remained closed.

"Something wrong?"

"Ah, no."

"Black Jack has started to behave," he said. "Guess you found the right mumbo jumbo, hocus-pocus, voodoo thing?"

Now, why when *he* said it did she hear respect instead of ridicule?

She moved to the back of the chair again and layered the top. Tamping down her frantic pulse, she concentrated on his question. "No magic spell. I think Black Jack has just realized I'm not out to hurt him. He knows he's safe here and it's okay to trust me."

Landon pulled in a long breath, his shoulders widening. A long silence stretched between them while he slowly released it. Her words replayed in her head. Was she talking about the horse or Landon?

"Enough about me. Why don't you tell me about you?" Maggie asked.

"There's nothing to tell."

"Oh, there must be something. All we know about you is that you've traveled around a lot and your best friend is a horse. What about your family?"

"My folks are gone."

"You mentioned your brother's ranch—"

"Are you finished yet?"

Her hands stilled, then she stepped away. "All done."

Landon rose and headed into the cabin. "Thanks, appreciate it."

Maggie doubted he meant it and bent to retrieve the scattered newspapers.

Should she follow? Hell, it was her cabin, and she needed to put this stuff in the trash. Marching inside, she laid the scissors and comb on the table and found the garbage can, then went to stand in front of the sink. He caught her staring while he looked at himself in the mirror. His gaze returned to his reflection and he pushed his hair back over his ears. "It looks great. I haven't had it this short since—" His lips pressed together. He swallowed before his eyes again met hers in the mirror. "—since I left home more than four years ago."

Maggie stepped in behind him. "You've been moving from ranch to ranch for the last four years?"

He leaned against the sink, his hands braced on his hips. "Must be hard for a homebody like you to understand, huh?"

"I think you're a homebody, too. I think you miss Still Waters—"

"What makes you think that's my home?"

"Okay, so it's your brother's," she conceded. "But I think you miss it, and your family."

He froze. "What family?"

"Your brother." Maggie paused, swiping her tongue over dry lips. "Your daughter?"

A tortured look filled his eyes. "You heard me in the barn with Anna."

She nodded then moved closer. "I'm sorry I made you think I didn't—"

"You heard wrong." Landon pushed away, and skirted past her. "I don't have a daughter."

"But Anna was looking at something." Maggie grabbed his arm, stopping him. "A picture? She asked you who—"

"Sara." The word was choked and grief stricken. "Her name was Sara. She's dead."

Shock and anguish rose inside her, bringing with it a fear only a parent could understand. "Oh, Landon, I'm sorry. I don't know what to say. I didn't mean to…I can't imagine how it feels to lose—dammit, this is none of my business. If you want me to shut up, just say so."

Landon spun back, sorrow etched over his face. He pulled her hard against his chest. His mouth hovered over hers and his fingers dug into her waist. "Maggie, shut up."

His gentle yet desperate words washed over her. Going on instinct, she didn't stop to think. Comfort. She wanted to comfort this man for what had to be unfathomable heartache. She cradled his face in her hands, and he closed his eyes. Her heart teetered on the edge of something sharp and painful. Her eyelids lowered and her lips moved to his—

A petrifying scream filled the air. Their eyes flew open. Puzzlement, then understanding filled his dark gaze.

"Anna!"

Landon and Maggie bumped into each other as they ran from the bathroom, racing onto the front porch, scanning the backyard.

"Anna!" She grabbed his shirt, repeating her daughter's name. "That was Anna!"

Another shrill cry filled the air, this time more animal than human. A cloud of dust billowed at the edge of the barn and Landon ran toward it. Raw, primal fear grabbed at him, making it feel as if he were pushing his way through waist-deep water.

He arrived at Black Jack's corral with Maggie just behind him. The wild mustang charged in a circle around the enclosure, kicking up dirt and rocks over himself and the scared little girl frozen in the middle. The tiny kitten in her arms wasn't faring any better.

"Stay back," Landon shouted at Nana B., who burst from the house.

Anna spotted Maggie and cried, "Mama!"

Maggie started forward, but Landon stopped her. "Anna, be quiet," he called out to her daughter.

"I'm—I'm scared." Her high-pitched voice crawled inside him, twisting his gut.

"I know you are, honey," Landon said.

Maggie's hands dug into his arms in a desperate need to be free, but rushing the corral would only make matters worse. "But you have to stay real still, like a statue."

"B-but the horse—"

"Shhh, no words, no movement, okay?"

Anna's head jerked in what he hoped was a nod. Landon doubted she'd be able to do what he asked for long. He looked at Maggie, the fear and shock in her eyes tearing at him. "Go to the far side, talk to Black Jack."

He gripped her arms. He had to make sure she understood. "Listen to me. Do your magic, cast a spell, hypnotize the beast, I don't care. Give the horse something to concentrate on besides Anna."

Maggie's eyes cleared except for the unmistakable gleam of unshed tears. "What are you—"

"I'll get Anna." He pushed her away. "Go."

Landon waited until Maggie headed in the other direction, her singsong voice wobbling as she called to the agitated animal. Black Jack reared in her direction, but he continued to dart between Anna and the railing.

With the horse's attention diverted, Landon crouched low

and inched toward the corral. He froze when Black Jack whipped in his direction, nostrils flaring as if catching his scent. Maggie's lyrical voice continued. The stallion turned his attention back to her, and Landon had to move.

Now.

Staying out of the animal's line of sight, he crawled to the fence and slipped between the posts. Maggie's voice caught, but his focus stayed on Anna.

He had to get to her. Save her.

In three steps, he grabbed her and the kitten, pulling both to his chest. The kitten's tiny claws dug into his arm. Anna's squeal alerted Black Jack again. The animal whirled.

Landon locked eyes with the creature, then raced back to the fence. He beat the charging horse by a heartbeat, diving through the posts. Hitting the dirt with his shoulder and hip, he rolled to his back, keeping his small charges safely tucked in his arms.

"Anna!"

"Mommy!"

Seconds later, his arms were empty as Anna hurled herself at Maggie.

Landon stared at the bright-blue sky. His breath came in short, hard gasps. He pushed up to a sitting position, ignoring the dig of pebbles and dirt in his skin. The kitten was safe in Nana B.'s hands and Anna in Maggie's.

Sharp throbbing pain shot across his lower back. Tears stung his eyes. He brushed the moisture away, blaming it on the swirl of dust covering him. He refused to believe it was the sight of three generations of a family in a tight huddle, Maggie's and Nana B.'s hands fluttering over Anna, from her ponytails to her sneakers.

She was okay. One child saved.

One child lost.

The feminine voices, fragile and shaking, faded into a loud buzz. A wall of darkness closed in. His heart pounded against his rib cage, threatening to explode. Panic rioted within, and one thought raced through his head.

Get out.

Now.

Ignoring the blinding pain in his back, he stumbled to the rear of the barn, feeling the lick of a searing inferno on his skin—flames engulfing wood, the snap and crackle screaming in his ears, soot blanketing his eyes, making it impossible to see.

Desperate to rid himself of the heat and pain, he wrenched on the outdoor faucet. The hose sprang to life. He bent over, braced a hand against his knee and doused himself in the cold spray.

He squeezed his eyes tight and water rushed over his neck and head, soaking the collar of his shirt and flattening the sleeves to his arms. It wasn't enough. His skin still burned. He yanked the shirt off and icy water bathed him in coldness, numbing him from the outside until it matched the deadened interior of his soul.

"I'm sorry, Sara," he cried, the useless apology falling from his lips. "I'm sorry, baby. I couldn't save…"

"Landon."

He heard her call his name, but it was too late. He didn't get to her in time. Either of them.

"Landon."

The heat of a hand on his arm jerked him upright. Water flew from his hair as he stumbled backward. He tunneled his fingers over his scalp, sending cold rivulets down his chest and back. His eyes, wide and unblinking, stared at nothing. "Don't—don't touch me."

"My god, are you all right?"

"I'm sorry." His voice cracked, and he struggled to get the words past the burn in his throat. "I—I couldn't do it. I couldn't save her."

"Landon, what are you talking about? You did save her. You saved Anna."

He blinked and saw his wife's cropped black hair plastered to her head, the light fading from her dark eyes, their child cradled in her arms.

I'm sorry, she whispered, *I'm sorry.*

"No." He brushed away her apology. "It's my fault. The flames, the smoke—it was too hot. I couldn't…I didn't get to you in time—"

"Landon, stop! I'm fine, Anna's fine." She grabbed his arms and tried to shake him. "What's the matter? What's wrong?"

"A-Anna?"

"She's fine. She's with my grand—Landon?"

He blinked again. The image before him shifted. Long, blond hair and green eyes came into focus. Bright sunshine on a hot summer day replaced the smoky gloom. "Mag—Maggie?"

"Yes, it's me. You saved my daughter—"

"But not mine." The words tore from his throat. "I couldn't save Sara."

"What are you talking about?"

The hose fell from his hand into the large puddle at their feet. He tore free of her hold. His chest heaved, drawing in life-giving breaths, while his mind allowed the nightmare to fade.

Three steps had his back against the corral. "Leave me alone."

"Landon, please." She advanced, concern in her eyes.

He spun away. It was a mistake. Naked to the waist, he'd bared his scars to her, the constant reminder of his failure.

"Ohmigod, what—Landon, what happened to you?"

He grabbed the top railing, the wood biting into his palms. His muscles flexed and pulled at the tight skin, the pain gone. Still, he flinched when her fingertips pressed lightly between his shoulder blades.

"There was a fire."

The words fell from his mouth, but it was as if someone else were speaking. He tried to stop, but they continued to flow. "It was nighttime, dark…so dark. My wife and d-daughter were trapped. I tried to find them, but by the time I got…got them out…it was too late. They died and it was my fault."

She put both hands on him as she moved up behind him. The softness of her hair caressed his skin, and a deep shudder coursed through him. The light touch of her lips to his back almost dropped him to his knees. He couldn't make out her murmured words, but he knew what she was offering.

Sympathy.

He didn't deserve it. Not now. Not from her.

He pushed her away, vaulted over the fence and started across the field. He whistled for G.W., who raced toward him.

"Landon, wait!" Maggie cried. "I want—I want to help."

"You can't." He swung onto his horse bareback, refusing to look at her. "No one can."

It was midnight when Maggie pulled her pickup to a stop at the house. All was dark but for the familiar back-porch light and the full moon.

She'd called home a few times during her shift at the bar to check on her daughter. Nana B. assured her Anna was fine and was more concerned about Black Jack being punished. Maggie knew it wasn't the horse's fault. She prayed the commotion hadn't set back the stallion's progress.

She had no idea if she could say the same about Landon.

She'd watched him take off across the open field, G.W. jumping the fencing to disappear over a hill. Nana B. had checked the foreman's cabin a few times, but it remained empty. Willie had stopped by the bar after dinner and told her Landon still hadn't returned. Maggie had been so worried about him, she had a hell of a time keeping her mind on her work. She'd screwed up more orders than she could count. All she could think about was Landon.

His reaction to saving Anna had scared her. He'd stood

before her like a man possessed, eyes wide and unseeing. She'd assured him Anna was okay. Then his second shocking confession fell from his lips when he said both his wife and child were dead—and he was to blame.

She had to find him. She had to tell him he was wrong. Landon was not a killer. There was no way he was responsible for anyone's death.

She stepped from the truck, untied the tail ends of her button-down, sleeveless denim shirt, and eyed the dark cabin across the pond. Relief filled her at the sight of his trailer and pickup parked along the side. Maybe he was home. If not, should she wait for Willie and then go looking for him?

Shoving her keys and wallet into the pocket of her miniskirt, she headed for the barn. First things first. She'd check to see if G.W. was back. If he was, she'd check on Landon.

Her boots crunched against the gravel as she walked inside the barn. A single overhead light cast a warm glow, but the stalls remained dark.

Caring so deeply about this wandering cowboy was wrong. In a matter of weeks, maybe days, he'd be heading down the road. Too bad her heart wasn't listening to her head. The same heart that was now lodged in her throat.

Please. Please let G.W. be here.

Tears of relief stung her eyes when the golden palomino swung his head over the stall door. Maggie wrapped her arms around his neck. "Oh, it's so wonderful to see you. Are you okay, sweetie? Where's your friend?"

"Right behind you."

Chapter Twelve

Maggie whirled around. Landon stood near the hayloft stairs, his white shirt hanging loose, hands shoved deep into the front of his jeans.

"You looking for me?"

His voice was low, but carried across the silent barn. The insolent tone changed her relief to anger.

"Damn straight, I am. What happened to you?"

"What do you mean?"

Maggie stomped across the floor. "I mean we were worried. The way you took off this afternoon. How could you do that?"

"Easy. I've been riding G.W. bareback for years." Landon uncrossed his boots and straightened. His cowboy hat cast a dark shadow over his face. "It's been a while, but you know what they say about never forgetting—"

"That's not what I'm talking about, dammit." Maggie smacked his chest with the palm of her hand. "How could you disappear? And for so long? There's a lot of desolate land out there. You or G.W. could've been injured with no way to call for help—"

Landon shrugged. "Who cares?"

"I do!"

Maggie smacked him again and this time he wrapped his hand around her wrist. The heat of his firm touch was her undoing. Tears filled her eyes. She wrenched free and flung herself at him, wrapping her arms around his neck.

"Oh, Landon, please tell me you're all right."

He stiffened, but Maggie refused to let go. A thrill raced through her as the hard planes of his body leveled against her curves. His hair was damp, and the sweet smell of soap and clean skin invaded her senses. It was forever before his hands touched her. A tingling shockwave raced over her skin when his fingertips, tentative at first, caressed her back. Then a groan rumbled in his chest and his hands tightened.

Maggie pressed her face to the warmth of his neck, not caring he'd be able to feel the wetness of her tears. "I was so scared." Her words came out in a rushed whisper. She didn't stop to think but spoke from the heart. "I didn't know where you'd gone, if you were okay…if you were coming back…"

Her lips found their way along his jaw, over the hard stubble. It stung and she licked away the pain, tasting heated male skin. Maggie swiped her tongue along the smoothness of his full bottom lip.

A rush of warm breath greeted her. She pushed to her tiptoes and with an unnerving boldness, covered his lips with hers. She explored the recesses of his mouth, seeking him, craving him. He responded, and their mouths collided in a heart-stopping kiss. Then Landon tore free and pushed her away.

"Maggie, stop." His voice was laced with desperation.

Dazed, she rocked back on her heels. The only thing keeping her from stumbling was his tight hold on her hips. "What?"

"You shouldn't kiss me like that."

She looked up, gulping air as she struggled to catch her breath. Damn his hat! She couldn't see his face, but felt his eyes boring into her. "W-why?"

"I'm not into gratuitous sex."

Shocked, she stared at him. "What?"

"You know. I saved your daughter's life. Now you feel obligated—"

"Stop right there." Her hands clutched the front of his shirt. "If you think I want—I kissed you because of what you did today, you're wrong."

His mouth flattened. "Am I?"

"Yes. Landon, I want—my kissing you has nothing to do with saving Anna. I kissed you because of the way you make me feel. Dammit, *because* you make me feel."

He stepped forward, bringing his body back in contact with hers. "Is that all you want, Maggie? Kisses?"

She could see his dark eyes now and the array of emotions swirling there. Desire. Need. Passion. It'd been years since she'd seen this kind of naked yearning in a man's eyes. Not because of a husbandly obligation, or a desire for her land. But because he wanted her.

A tremor of fear coursed through her. She didn't know if she was ready for this. A moment ago, she was running on pure emotion, a need to be in this man's arms. What would tomorrow hold if they took this step tonight?

"Come on, Maggie." He moved closer, pressing her against the stair railing. He dipped his head and trailed his lips from her forehead to her cheek. "Say it. Tell me what you want."

She threw all her doubts aside. "You. I want you."

Landon swallowed the last of her declaration with his kiss.

She wanted him. And he wanted her.

Her hands clutched at his shoulders as she returned his deepening kiss. He tightened his arms in a viselike grip, needing to get her closer. It wasn't enough.

She was trying to undo his shirt with desperate, frantic movements. But he refused to allow the rest of their bodies to separate. The feel of her cradled between his thighs, against his erection, sent skyrockets exploding deep inside.

Her fingers yanked at the collar, and her gasp of surprise at how easy the materials parted made him chuckle.

"Snaps, darling," he whispered against her lips. "Go ahead, give it a tug."

Maggie complied and his shirt flew open. The cool night air hit the heat of his skin. Then the warmth of her touch from his collarbone to the too-tight waistband of his jeans sent his blood pounding through his veins.

"My turn." His fingers went to the top button of her shirt.

"Careful, cowboy. Those are regular buttons," she whispered, while laying soft kisses on his chest.

"I'll figure it out." His fingers fumbled with the first button and again with the second. Hell, it had been years since he'd taken off a woman's clothes. Years since he had been with a woman.

So why now? Why her?

He was saved from answering when Maggie's hands brushed his away. He watched as she undid the buttons herself. The familiar smells of her hard work at the bar drifted from her warm skin, not completely masking the fresh linen scent that was uniquely hers.

She hesitated after the last button, making no move to part her shirt. "Ah, it's…it's been a long time. I haven't done anything like this since my marriage ended. Long before my marriage ended, actually."

A territorial thrill he had no right to feel raced through Landon. He'd wondered if loneliness and need had caused her to find comfort in another's arms after her ex had walked out. The fact she hadn't made his mouth go dry.

"Me, too, darling." He captured her face in his hands, and

kept his gaze locked with her. He lowered his head, mixing kisses with his words. "Me, too."

There was surprise in her bright-green eyes as his mouth covered hers in a carnal kiss. Her hands dropped to his hips, her fingers caressing him. He peeled her shirt off her shoulders and pulled it away to see full breasts covered in white cotton.

"I know, it's nothing fancy." The tips of her fingernails bit into his skin as she tightened her grip. "It's plain, serviceable—"

"Perfect." Landon dropped his hands to her waist and lifted Maggie until she stood on the first step of the stairs. "You're perfect."

She grabbed his biceps, unable to raise her hands any higher, her shirt pinning her arms to her side. He let go long enough to push back the brow of his Stetson, his eyes never leaving the deep shadow of her cleavage. Thanks to the step, he had only to bend his head a little to place his mouth on the soft skin. His fingers wrapped around her back, while his thumbs brushed up and down her stomach from the waistband of her skirt to the underside of her breasts. Her heart beat wildly beneath his lips. He kissed a trail to her collarbone, loving how she bent toward him, her hair creating a curtain of privacy.

Was this happening? Did he have this woman—this responsive, amazing, beautiful woman in his arms? She arched into him, a low moan escaping when he covered her breasts with his hands. He swallowed the sound when he kissed her again.

She wanted to touch him. Everywhere. But all she could do was hold on as a whirl of emotions and long-unfed desires whipped her into a summertime storm, complete with thunder-like rumbles and rushing winds. The weight of his hands on her, the callused tips of his fingers as he traced the upper edge of her bra, sent an electric fizz zipping over her skin. His palms cupped and caressed while his mouth ravaged her in an endless kiss. His fingers moved upward, following the path of her bra straps. Her stomach clenched. He worked his way beneath the straps then inched them from her shoulders.

Whistling invaded her ears, an out-of-tune warble of a classic love-gone-wrong song.

Maggie tore her mouth from his. "Ohmigod, do you hear that?"

"What?" Landon's chest rose and fell, his words punched out between deep, gutted breaths.

"Whistling. Do you hear it?" Realization dawned. "Willie! He's heading in here!"

The creak of the barn door sounded like a shotgun to Maggie. Suddenly Landon lifted her into his arms. "Landon! What are you—"

"Shhh."

He took the stairs to the loft two at a time and rounded the corner, stepping into the darkness as Willie appeared below. Lowering her feet to the ground, he pressed her against the rough-hewn post at the landing. "We can't be seen," he whispered.

His body blocked her view, but Maggie could hear Willie's chatter below as he discovered Landon's horse back in its stall. "Let me go talk to him," she whispered back. "I don't want—"

"What's the matter, Maggie?" Landon moved closer, his body hard against hers. She could hear the teasing in his hushed voice. "Never been caught necking in the hayloft?"

"No, and I don't want to start now."

She tried to ignore the heat of his bare skin and the clean, manly smell of him mixed with the scent of fresh hay. Moonlight streamed through the open loft door, but here in the shadows it was dark. The feel of his lips on her neck made her jump, and his touch, high on her thighs beneath her skirt, forced a low, deep moan. "Landon!"

"Shhh, you don't want to be discovered. Remember?" His tongue teased her ear, leaving a wet heat on the edge.

Maggie tilted her head to the side and closed her eyes. She

struggled between letting this wonderful craziness continue and doing the right thing. "I still think—"

Before she could finish, Landon stripped her shirt from where it hung at her elbows. Shocked, her eyes flew open in time to see it sail into the dark corner of the loft.

"You think too much. How about just feel, Maggie?" His soft words floated over her. His hands caressed her bare skin from her shoulders to her fingertips. "Feel my lips on your face, my hands on your skin."

He dropped his hands again to her legs and lifted her skirt. His fingers curled around the back of her thighs and pressed his erection against her. "Feel what you do to me."

Maggie let his words wash over her. Delving her fingers into his damp hair, she pulled his mouth to hers, feeling his smile against her lips. Seconds later, she grabbed his Stetson and it, too, sailed across the loft.

"Hey!"

"Shhh." She repeated his words back to him, wishing she could see his face. "You think too much, too."

"That was the best thing you could think to remove?" he groaned, his fingers pressing into her flesh when Maggie's hips rotated against him.

"I want to see your face."

Landon stilled. "It's too dark up here."

"Not for this," she replied, fingers dancing over his forehead, outlining his brows and running over the hard planes of his cheeks. She traced his lips and he nipped at her finger, then soothed the bite with the tip of his tongue.

A snap sounded in the main barn and everything went dark. The creak of the barn door closing told her Willie had left. "Ah, it looks like we're alone again."

"Good."

Landon crashed his mouth on hers. Maggie tasted desperation in his kiss. A swirl of questions invaded her head, but she shut them out and focused on her body and soul. And what this one-of-a-kind cowboy was doing to both.

He didn't want to talk.

He didn't want to think.

He only wanted this woman. All of her.

A fine sheen of sweat broke out over his skin. He didn't know if it was from the summer heat or from having Maggie in his arms. He eased his kiss—the last thing he wanted was to hurt her—but she dug her fingertips into his shoulders and urged him onward.

Unable to stop the desire roaring inside, Landon ravished her mouth. He pulled her closer, his hands pushing her skirt higher until he cupped the bare skin of her backside.

Whoa, he never expected that.

His fingers outlined the barely-there pieces of silky string and a patch of lace. After seeing her bra, he'd figured on the same white cotton. Not that he had a problem with it. Hell, this woman could make a potato sack sexy. A groan ripped from his mouth, and the need to breathe made him pull back.

"Okay, so now you know my secret," Maggie panted, her words hot against his skin.

"You wear these all the time?" he asked.

"I threw out my plain granny-panties the day I signed my divorce papers." She kissed his neck, shoulders and chest. "Helps remind me I'm a woman while I'm mucking out stalls and chasing after horses."

She dragged his shirt over his shoulders, and he reluctantly let her go so she could tug it down his arms. It dropped to the ground. Her hands returned to his body, her blunt nails scraping against his muscles. They caught on his nipples, and a loud hiss escaped his lips.

"You like that?" she asked, repeating the movement, nicking the small nubs as she rained kisses on his chest.

"Yeah, I like it," he replied, one hand cupping the back of her head, while the other moved to her back. With a practiced motion, honed ages ago on the rodeo circuit, he released the clasp of her bra. The tentative stroke of her tongue across one of his nipples made him crazy, and he yanked her bra from her arms. She shivered as he dropped it to the floor and pulled her in tight.

"You cold?"

"No, not really…nervous, maybe."

Her soft words tugged at his heart. It was dark where they stood in the loft, more so now with the light shut off. It was hard to see her. And he wanted to. Wanted to see every inch of her. But first, he wanted her to be sure about this.

No man ever died from not finishing what he'd started, even if the ache took forever to go away. Hell, he'd never forced a woman, no matter how long it'd been. He needed to make sure this was what she truly wanted.

He bent, grabbed his shirt and shook it out. Pulling in a deep breath, he wrapped it around Maggie's shoulders, helping her to slide her arms into the sleeves. He pulled it closed over her breasts, his heart stopping in his chest when his hands brushed against her lush curves.

"Landon? What are you doing?"

"Taking a deep breath." He tried to smile, then realized it didn't matter. She couldn't see his face. He gave her fingers a squeeze. "Taking a few deep breaths."

"You're stopping?"

Was that disappointment in her voice? "We need a minute—"

"You've changed your mind." Her voice fell away and he could tell she'd dropped her chin to her chest. "You don't want me. I get it."

Anger surged through him. What in the hell was she talking about? How could she honestly think that? He grabbed her hand and gently pressed it over the rigid flesh straining against his jeans. "Not want you? Does this feel like a man who doesn't want you?"

Cradling her chin with his other hand, he forced her to look at him. Damn, he needed her to see his face. He rubbed his thumb back and forth across her lips, then gave in to the need to kiss her doubts away. He pressed his mouth to hers, easily pushing past her lips to deepen the kiss.

Maggie responded instantly, returning his kiss with a matched eagerness. She fervently stroked him through his jeans. Then her hands went to his waistband, and she tugged on the top button. It gave way. Seconds later, two more followed.

Landon tore his mouth from hers, his breath coming in harsh gasps. He rested his forehead against her. She freed the last few buttons. His hands met hers as they moved to the elastic waist of his briefs.

"I need to know you want this," he panted, "that you're sure."

"I want this, Landon." She punctuated each word with a tug on his jeans. They slid from his waist to his hips.

His knees buckled at the delicate touch of her fingertips as they inched inside his briefs. She reached low and captured him in the palm of her hand. Then she released him and skimmed the sides of his body until she wrapped her hands around his neck.

"I'm sure."

He pulled her hard against him. Her skin melted into his and he backed her farther into the loft among the towering stacks of hay.

He stopped when they were bathed in moonlight, and with one hand, forced her to look at him. "Say it again."

"I want this," she repeated, looking at him. "I want you."

Her blond hair, silver in the moonlight, shaded her eyes. But not enough to hide her certainty. Along with something else. He didn't have time to decipher it before she closed her eyes and arched her back, her breasts sliding over his skin. "Landon, please…"

He caught her plea in a quick kiss, then bent and captured the beaded tip of one breast in his mouth. He suckled, nipped and wet it with the heat of his tongue. His hands pushed her skirt up to her waist, covering the tight perfection of her backside. She rocked against him, hot and wet through the scrap of lace covering her.

He needed that wetness on his hands, his fingers inside her.

They tangled in the strings of her panties, and he pushed the lace aside, his thumb exploring the soft curls until he found her center. The slightest pressure brought forth a sweet moan from Maggie and both their knees buckled.

He released her nipple with a reverent kiss. He had to get them horizontal. "I don't know how soft the hay is—"

"Behind you," Maggie gasped, pushing at his shoulders. "A horse blanket."

Landon turned. The faded quilt lay over a short stack of hay. He pulled her to the bale and tumbled down, tugging her with him.

She grabbed his shoulders as he pulled her onto his lap. With a hushed squeal, her knees collapsed, the toes of her boots catching at the edge of the hay bale. "Landon, I'm going to fall."

"No way," he growled against her skin as he caught her, his mouth caressing the swell of her breasts. "I won't let you."

Too late.

She'd already fallen hard and fast. There was nothing she could do to stop it. And she didn't want to. She had no idea what was going to happen after tonight, and—for once—it was okay she didn't care. She was determined to live in the here and now, in this moment, with this man.

Maggie stretched higher, cradling Landon's head in her hands. He covered her breasts in more wet kisses and his fingers continued to caress her. She trembled under his touch, her breath disappearing from her lungs. The cotton material of his shirt clung to her sweat-dampened skin. She wanted it off, but at the same time loved the feel of it wrapped around her. The denim of his jeans scraped her inner thighs.

When he slid one finger deep inside her, she arched off his lap. Her body convulsed and a tightening curled in her chest, ready to explode. It had been so long. She wasn't going to last.

She forced Landon to look at her. "No, not like this."

"Yes." His lips brushed over hers. "Yes, like this."

Her fingers gripped the powerful muscles of his shoulders. It was too potent, too overwhelming, but every inch of her body reveled in it. She'd never felt this way before. Strong and weak, generous and needy. She wanted to give all of herself and take everything. His lips left a trail of kisses over her collarbone, his uneven breaths matching hers. He found his way back to her mouth. His tongue stroking and demanding, mimicking his fingers on the most intimate part of her, creating a burning intensity that rose higher and higher, thrusting her to the edge of a cavernous void.

Then his hand was gone and he filled her with his hard length in one smooth motion. She had no idea how he'd managed it, but he was inside her. His arms encircling her, his kiss swallowing her cries when she shattered around him. She tore her mouth from him, her head dropping back as her body leapt into the emptiness to find it filled with explosions of fire and heat.

She welcomed his commanding thrusts, and his raw, passion-filled moans thrilled her inexperienced heart. He drove them deeper into a passionate haze until his guttural groan filled the air and he found his own release. Shivers, sparked by uncontrollable joy, danced along her skin. Catching her breath was impossible until the wild race of her heart slowed to a powerful thump, thump, thump. She cradled his head in her arms and dropped a tender kiss on his sweat-soaked forehead.

He pulled her close, then stilled. His viselike grip on her back eased.

"I…" Chest heaving, he struggled to catch his breath. "I guess this is where…where I should apologize."

Chapter Thirteen

Maggie went still in his arms. Then she was off his lap in a shot. She yanked her skirt down around her sexy backside and silky thighs before finding her shirt and bra.

He licked his suddenly dry lips. "Let me explain—"

"Not necessary," Maggie interrupted. "I think your need to apologize says enough."

Damn, how could she walk? He couldn't even stand—his legs were like jelly. Settling instead for tucking himself back into his briefs, he managed to get his jeans up to where they belonged. He stopped fighting with his fly to grab her as she marched past him.

He forced her to sit on the bale of hay and knelt at her feet. "Maggie—"

"No explanation needed." Avoiding his eyes, she grabbed at the shirt she still had on—*his shirt*—and pulled it tight over her breasts. "I get it."

"No, you don't. I know what's running through your head, and you can stop right now."

"You have no idea what I'm—"

"I didn't use protection."

Maggie froze. The clothing in her hands fell to her lap, eyes wide.

Damn, damn, and double damn!

This wasn't like him. Since his first time, barely into his teens, he'd never forgotten. Hell, it was years before he knew what it felt like to be inside a woman, flesh to flesh.

Landon stood up. He realized he had Maggie's torn panties in his grasp and shoved them in his pocket then backed away. Her eyes followed his every move.

A sudden desire to find his hat filled him. He spotted it nearby, grabbed it and shoved on his head. "I'm sorry, it never crossed—but you don't have to worry. About me, I mean. I meant it when I said it's been a while. I'm clean. I got a complete physical before I got—" He saw the shadow of a smile on her face. "Are you laughing at me?"

"No." Her gaze flew to his. "No, I would never laugh. I thought... So, you weren't going to apologize because I wasn't—because it wasn't good?"

"Maggie, it was so good, I'm already hard again."

Desire flashed in her eyes.

Landon yanked his hat farther down his forehead, not wanting her to see the same mirrored in his. "But that's not important—"

"It's okay."

"You're damn right it was. Better than okay."

"I mean *it's* okay. You don't have to worry about me getting preg—" One hand flattened low over her belly, the other fisted at her side, bunching the faded quilt. "I'm on birth control."

A one-two sucker punch crashed into Landon, knocking all the air from his lungs. An image flashed in his head. Maggie pregnant with their baby. His child growing inside her.

No.

He slammed his eyes closed, shattering the picture into a

thousand pieces. Another child was the last thing he needed. Or wanted. He'd already learned his lesson, in the most gut-wrenching way possible. He wasn't cut out to be a father. He never wanted to be responsible for another human life ever again.

"Landon?"

He jerked when the warmth of her hand landed against his bare skin. He opened his eyes to find her standing in front of him. Her other hand held the quilt tight around her shoulders. It covered her completely from her chin to her boots. His body blocked the moonlight, leaving her face in shadow.

"Did you hear what I said?" she asked.

Her words blew hot across his skin, and his need for this woman roared back to life. He jammed his hands into his back pockets to keep from reaching for her. "Ah, yeah…birth control. I heard you."

She nodded, her long hair, mussed from his hands, swaying against her cheeks. "You don't have to worry about the other thing. I'm clean, too. I mean, I haven't been with anyone since Al—after I learned about my ex's numerous affairs. I made sure I got tested."

A rage, nothing to do with sexual want, pressed hard in his stomach. "Your ex is the biggest jackass in the county. Hell, the whole state of Wyoming."

A smile came to her full lips. "You know, talk like that will get you…" Her voice held a teasing hint before it trailed off.

"What?" Landon pushed her jerk of an ex-husband from his mind. He took a step toward her, forcing her to tilt her head back in order not to break eye contact. "What will I get, Miss Maggie?"

Her shoulder squared and she lifted her chin. "Me. Again. Now. If you want—"

He whipped his hands out from behind him to cup her face, his kiss cutting off her words. *He did want.*

He pushed his tongue past her open lips, the heat inside

adding to his spiraling need for this woman. She stilled under his assault and he immediately pulled back. The last thing he wanted was to scare her.

Sipping softly at the outer corners of her lips, he struggled to clamp down on his intense passion. He had no idea where it came from. He should tell her no. He should walk away.

He couldn't.

"I want you," he whispered, the hoarseness in his voice betraying his hunger. "Again. I want to lay with you between the cool sheets in that big old brass bed. I want to feel your body draped over mine. I want to be so deep inside you, we won't be able to tell where I end and you begin."

She swayed into him and he scooped her into his arms, blanket, clothes and all, and started for the loft stairs.

"I can walk, you know." She released the blanket, letting it fall from her shoulders as she wrapped her arms around his neck.

Her shirt parted and the feel of her breasts against his chest made him almost miss the last step. He tightened his hold as they exited the barn, thankful the moon had skipped behind the clouds.

"I can walk faster," he said roughly.

He wasn't sure, but Landon thought he'd felt her lips curve into a smile against his neck.

Maggie snuggled into the pillow. She pulled in a deep breath, filling her head with the sexy smell of pure man. The man beside her asleep on his stomach, his face half hidden by the silkiness of his hair.

She smiled. His scent covered her everywhere. Her hair, her skin—

She closed her eyes and relived the past hours with him, making love in the hayloft and twice more after they got to the cabin. The memory of the passion between them caused her to shiver. She burrowed beneath the sheets, blaming the cool breeze that came through the window.

Maggie opened her eyes again, noticing how the light of the coming dawn was slowly chasing away the darkness. She should get back to the main house. But she didn't want to leave. Not yet.

She concentrated on Landon again. Using her fingertips, she traced the corded muscles of his bicep, followed the hills and valleys to the bend of his elbow. She moved to his back, his strength evident even as he slept, her fingers slipping toward his tapered waist. The hard ridge of puckered scar tissue made her pause. Tears filled her eyes as his words returned to her.

A fire.

Wife and d-daughter trapped inside.

They died.

My fault.

Her eyes overflowed and the tears ran down her cheek, disappearing into the fabric of the pillowcase. He'd been hurt trying to save them. The thought of losing her family stabbed Maggie deeply.

How had he survived? Was he still in pain?

Of course he was.

Flashes from the past few weeks filled her head. The morning he'd fallen to his knees after fixing her corral. The stiffness in his walk after he saved Hank. The time he'd stumbled after his sudden rise from the porch. It had nothing to do with the beers he'd drunk and everything to do with scars her fingers massaged.

"Don't."

Maggie's gaze flew to Landon's face. His eyes remained closed, mouth pulled tight. "Am I hurting you?"

After a long moment, he shook his head.

She rose on one elbow, holding the sheet to her breasts. Leaning closer, she kneaded the inflexible scars. They stood out against the darkness of his skin, but she could tell they weren't new.

How long had he carried the physical and psychological pain of that horrific night?

"Tell me," she whispered, refusing to let him pull away despite his attempts. Moving the sheet low on his hips, she continued to stroke his skin, feeling the hard muscles beneath begin to respond. "Please, tell me what happened to you…to them."

Long minutes passed before he spoke. "After my parents died, I was in charge of running my family's ranch—"

"Still Waters." Maggie's breath caught as she realized the ranch his brother worked for, one of the biggest and most profitable in Texas, belonged to Landon. To him and his family.

He nodded and continued, "Business took me away a lot. Meetings, deal making, contracts…hell, I spent more time in office buildings than on the land. And it wasn't going well. The weather, a couple of stupid moves on my part—"

His shoulders expanded as he pulled in a deep breath before slowly releasing it. "To top it off, my so-called marriage wasn't a happy one. We married because of…circumstances, not love. Jenna wanted more of my time than I could give, so she found company elsewhere. Not hard to do on a ranch full of cowboys."

Landon's hands clenched the pillow beneath his head, crushing its softness in his tight grip. "I was going to end it. Then she told me she was pregnant. I didn't know if the baby was mine, and after Sara was born, I insisted on a paternity test. She was a Cartwright. I tried to make the marriage work, but Jenna didn't care…about me or the baby."

Maggie's eyes closed, trapping more tears. Her heart broke for him and his little girl. She didn't want to judge the woman, but how could Landon's wife not be satisfied with him? He was strong and hardworking, patient and kind.

"One night I was late getting home. I saw the fire from the main road. By the time I got there, one of the old horse barns was completely engulfed. My men and I were so busy trying to save the horses and control the flames no one noticed it had spread to the second story of the main house. By the time we did, the top floor was… I raced inside. It took me forever, but I found her…them—"

His voice broke and Landon jerked from the bed.

Maggie's eyes flew open. She watched silently as he yanked open a dresser drawer and pulled out fresh clothes. Pain and sorrow emanated from him as he tugged on his underwear and jeans. She wanted so badly to go to him, to hold him in her arms.

"I am so sorry for your loss," she said, knowing it was inadequate.

"Yeah, my loss." Landon paced in front of the long table separating the main room from the kitchen. "I brought it on myself. I did this!"

"Landon, no!" Maggie grabbed at the T-shirt he'd tossed on the bed. She pulled it over her head, thankful it fell past her naked backside. Turning on the bedside lamp, she went to him. "You can't blame your—"

"I should've been there." He pulled from her touch and walked to the window, his gaze focused on the outside world. "It was my fault. It doesn't matter how it started, or what any damn report said. I was—" He crossed his arms over his chest and faced her, his expression lost in the darkness. "I am responsible."

Maggie ached for him. His grief was so powerful it surrounded him like a living thing, sucking all the life from the room. The tragedy explained so many questions that had been swirling inside her since she'd met him.

Only he wasn't a wandering cowboy, despite what he'd told them about working at other ranches. He was the owner of a spread five times the size of the Crescent Moon, and he'd walked away from it all.

"When did it happen?" she asked.

"Five years ago," he answered in a hushed whisper. "Sara would have been seven come November."

"So you walked away? Left your home?"

His gaze dropped.

She sensed that something deep inside him kept him from telling her the full truth. He'd already said too much. "Yes… and no."

"What does that mean?"

He stared at the floor for a long time then drew in a deep breath before looking at her again. "It means it doesn't matter. It's in the past."

"Landon—"

"Look, you wanted to know about my scars and I told you." His voice became hard. "I've satisfied your curiosity about my past. You know every—all you need to know."

He heard the words coming from his mouth, and while he silently cursed every one of them, they had to be said.

He couldn't believe he'd spilled his guts to her. What the hell had made him—no, he knew why. Maggie. She was getting too close. Her, her family and this whole damn place.

He moved past her, waving at the rumpled blankets on the bed. "Don't think what happened here changes anything. I made it clear from the beginning this was a temporary job."

Her face paled as she grabbed her clothes and boots and disappeared into the bathroom. Landon cursed. He never should've gone to the barn tonight.

He never should've touched her.

Hell, it was inevitable. He'd known the moment he offered to work here something like it would happen. But a wild, uncontrollable coming together in the hayloft was one thing. Then he'd brought her here, and it had changed from sex to something more. Holding her, loving her, letting her love him. He'd never felt this way in his entire life. And he didn't deserve it.

Plus, Maggie and her family didn't deserve to have an ex-con in their life. Being cleared of the crime didn't free him of the responsibility. He'd failed to protect his family and he could never take that chance again.

Fully dressed, Maggie walked from the bathroom and held out his T-shirt. "Don't worry about the sheets. As you know, we do the laundry around here on Mondays."

He took the shirt. "Maggie—"

"Don't." She stopped at the door, her hand on the knob. "I don't know what switch I pulled or why talking about your past is causing you to be this way—"

Her voice broke, and a hard knot of guilt settled in Landon's stomach. He couldn't stop himself from walking up behind her. The stiffness in her shoulders told him not to touch her. He twisted the shirt in his fists, using every ounce of his resolve to obey.

"I know I should agree with you and say this doesn't change anything between us. Not that there is anything…" Her voice was so low it was barely a whisper.

Landon tried to concentrate on what she was saying, but something—something was wrong. "Maggie, stop talking."

She whirled around. "How dare you—"

Landon silenced her. His head buzzed with memories of that horrific night. That had to be it. That had to be why the crackle of flames filled his ears and a deep breath brought with it the rancid smell of—

Smoke!

He pushed her out of the way and yanked open the door, eyes flying over the main house, the barn and bunkhouse. Nothing. He scanned the area again, another deep breath bringing with it the taste and smell of a smoldering fire. The predawn lightening of the sky mixed so well with the swirls of gray and white he missed it the first time.

"The tool shed." He spun around and grabbed his boots. He pulled them on and yanked the shirt Maggie had worn earlier over his head. "It's on—"

"Fire!"

Willie's hoarse cry carried across the yard. Maggie raced outside, Landon right behind her. He wanted to tell her to stay back, but it would be useless. He watched as Willie, dressed in a wrinkled wife-beater, boxers and boots, grabbed the hose attached to the bunkhouse.

Racing for the hose behind the barn, he gave a quick prayer, thankful the tool shed stood apart from the other buildings. He twisted the spigot and aimed the rushing water at the engulfed structure.

The heat licked at his skin and he was transported instantly to the scorching inferno of another fire. Another night.

He snapped back to the present, and the seductive dance of the flames, twisting and spiraling into the sky, taunted him as they devoured every square inch of the shed. The crackle of the wood jeered his inability to advance, to breathe, to fight back.

He couldn't move.

Chapter Fourteen

"Willie, wet the grass," Maggie yelled, her hands covering Landon's unmoving fingers. She twisted the hose, stealing it from his grasp and shoved him out of the way with her hip.

"Get a shovel from the barn," she shouted over her shoulder. "We need a firebreak to keep from losing the paddocks."

She stared into his wide, dark eyes. The fresh memory of what he'd told her about his family was all over his face. Bottomless pain and sadness contorted his features. She hoped he understood the compassion and empathy in hers.

"Go," she added softly. He blinked hard and pulled himself from the blaze's hypnotic hold.

"Don't get too close," he said. "You're not dressed properly—get yourself wet."

Maggie's heart tripped at the concern in his voice. She turned the hose into the air and doused them both with a spray of cold water before directing it at the base of the fire.

Landon ran for the barn, reaching it just as Hank's pickup

circled around from the back. "What the damnation is going on?" he asked, hopping from the truck's cab.

"Come with me," Landon commanded.

Within minutes, the two of them emptied the barn, setting the horses loose in the pasture. Then they went to work creating a circle of turned earth around the burning structure, ensuring that it would be the only thing on the ranch consumed by the flames.

Nana B. appeared on the side porch, her arms around Anna, both in their pajamas. Hank took the hose from Willie with orders for him to get inside and get some clothes on his skinny bones.

"Here, give me that." Landon reached for the hose in Maggie's hand.

She stepped away, her gaze focused on the burning embers and spots of flame. "I'm fine. I can do this."

"I know you can." He grabbed the hose. "Please…let me. Besides, I saw Nana B. with the phone to her ear. I bet your friend the sheriff is going to show up any minute."

Maggie looked over at the porch, her heart breaking at the fear on her grandmother's and Anna's faces. She longed to go to them, but she had to be certain Landon was okay, too. "Are you sure?" she asked.

"Yes, I'm sure." His hand covered hers, his touch cool and wet for a moment before he pulled away and took the hose. "It's pretty much under control anyway."

What he said was true. Hank stood on the far side of the structure, still dousing the wood with rushing water. The fire was more smoke than flames now. She could see through the smoldering building to her cowboy's ragged features.

"And you might want to get out of those wet clothes," he said distantly. "Before your grandmother figures out you didn't sleep in them or your own bed last night."

His tone of voice was a stark reminder of what he'd said inside his cabin. He'd shut down, physical and emotionally, for reasons she couldn't comprehend. And now that another crisis had been averted, he was doing it again.

Maggie gave a powerful tug with the crowbar and blinked back the fresh sting of tears. She wouldn't cry. Not out here in broad daylight. At night, alone in her bed, was another story.

It had been three days since the fire. By the time Destiny's volunteer fire department had arrived, the shed was a total loss. Gage had called this morning and confirmed the initial findings. An electrical short in the new wiring. He then gave her the okay to clear the site.

She was determined to start the rebuilding right away. It was going to put a dent in her savings, but she didn't have any choice. Besides, it felt good to destroy what remained of the charred wooden structure. Anna said it was giving her nightmares. Maggie had to admit the blackened skeletal remains made it tough for her to get any rest as well. Better to blame the fire than the real reason for her sleepless nights.

A six-foot walking tower of stone silence.

Landon had gone from passionate lover to distant employee in a matter of just a few hours. She'd tried to find a private moment to talk, but she wasn't sure what she'd say if she found it.

I'm sorry? Sorry for asking about your past? Sorry for throwing myself in your arms? Sorry for being stupid enough to give my heart to a man who can't—or won't—take it?

Yes, she'd fallen in love with the wrong man. Again.

A man who'd effectively shut her out, willing to suffer her presence only when she was talking about the ranch. He rarely looked her in the eye, his damn hat always pulled low over her brow. When he spoke, it was all business, with barely a "yes, ma'am" or "no, ma'am" to her questions.

One final tug and the shed's last corner stud fell to the ground at her feet. There. Much better.

Liar.

She didn't have any idea how to make things better. Around the ranch. Or with Landon.

"Lord, it's said you never give a body more than they can handle." Maggie spoke the prayer softly as she added the dead wood to the pile. "But if it's all the same, I think I'm at my limit."

"Excuse me, Miss Maggie?"

Startled, Maggie whirled around at the voice. Surprise filled her at the sight of Spence Wilson and Charlie Bain, her former employees. She hadn't heard the sound of Spence's battered pickup. Both stood with their hats in their hands and sheepish looks on their faces as they tried to keep their gaze off the pile of burnt rubble.

"What are you doing here?" Thankful she'd remembered her bandanna this morning, she used it to erase the moisture from her eyes.

"We've been talking it over and well…these are for you." Spence thrust a bouquet of yellow roses wrapped in green tissue at her.

Maggie dropped the crowbar and grabbed at the flowers before they landed in the dirt. "Oh, ah…thank you."

Spence glanced over at Charlie who looked very interested in the toes of his cowboy boots. "We'd like to come back to the Crescent Moon. If you'll have us."

Maggie gripped the flowers, schooling her features not to reveal her shock. Almost a month since they'd walked out and no one had answered any of her ads. Except for Landon.

She pushed the thought aside. "Why?"

"Greeley's money was nice, but lately we've heard talk. How he's looking to break you and take your land." Spence's gaze shot to the pile of rubble from the shed and then back to Maggie. "What Greeley's doing ain't right, and we don't want any part of it."

"Besides, the cook at the Triple G doesn't come anywhere close to Nana B.'s fixings," Charlie added with a small grin.

Optimism welled inside of her. Spence and Charlie knew how things worked around the ranch. It wouldn't take long for them to learn the changes Landon made. They could take on some of the heavy work he tended to keep from Hank and Willie.

"We know you got yourself a new foreman," Spence said, putting his hat back on his head. "The place is looking good. But your ads are still up around town, so if you're interested—"

Another truck rounded the corner and pulled to a stop near them. Hank was at the wheel with Willie and Landon next to him. Landon opened the passenger door and stepped out, his gaze firmly planted on Spence and Charlie.

Maggie ignored the crazy jump her heart took at the sight of him, standing there in dusty jeans, sweat-soaked T-shirt and familiar black Stetson.

"What's going on?" he said.

She quickly made introductions, telling herself it didn't matter Landon couldn't look at her.

Willie climbed out of the truck, leaving the passenger door open. "What are you young pups doing here?" he said. "Got yourselves free of Greeley's leash?"

"Spence and Charlie work here…again," Maggie said, pleased to see the happiness on their faces.

"Since when?" Landon asked.

"Since now."

Landon crossed his arms over his chest. His gaze never left the younger men, both of whom tried their best not to squirm under his direct stare.

"Why don't you two go into town with Hank?" Maggie said to Spence and Charlie. "You can put away your gear later."

"Yes ma'am," they said in unison and headed for the pickup.

Willie moved away, but Landon stood his ground, forcing them to walk around him. Irritation cut through Maggie, but she kept her mouth shut until the pickup pulled away and disappeared down the drive.

"Want to explain your behavior?" she demanded.

Landon remained silent. A muscle twitched in his cheek.

"That is, if you can put together more than a two-word sentence."

Willie ducked his head and headed for the barn. "I think I'll find something to keep me busy."

"Well?" Maggie asked, after Willie was out of earshot.

"You sure about this?"

Wow. Four words strung together. She struggled to rein in her temper, knowing her reasons for being angry with Landon went much deeper than the way he was questioning her hiring skills.

"Yes. I've known those guys a long time and they're good people. I'm glad to have them back because now I can concentrate on Black Jack."

"I thought things were going okay with the beast."

"They are—they were—before the fire. He's been a bit skittish since then. It's gonna take some time for him to trust me again." Maggie knew she was talking about Landon as much as the horse. Would he see that?

He nodded. "You've been busy this morning."

"Gage called. He said the fire was due to faulty wiring. They're sending a report to the manufacturer." She had to make sure Landon didn't think this was his or Willie's mistake. "I know you two installed it, but it passed inspection."

"I'm sorry about the fire."

"It's nobody's fault."

"I know." Landon paused. "You want it rebuilt right away?"

"Yes, especially now with Spence and Charlie back." Maggie waved the flowers at the bunkhouse. "Keeping the tools in the bunkhouse was a temporary solution, and with three full-time cowboys living there now—"

"Temporary isn't going to work, is it?"

She stopped and looked at him. "No, it isn't."

"Maggie—"

A Jeep rounded the corner and pulled into the drive, cutting off whatever Landon was going to say. The sheriff's emblem on the door gleamed in the bright sunlight. It came to a stop near the house and Leeann stepped out, dressed in her summer khaki uniform.

"You were saying?" Maggie pushed.

"You've got company." Landon turned and headed for the cabin.

"What in tarnation are you doing?"

Landon paused at the sound of Willie's voice then continued to shove his clothes into the duffel bags on the bed. "Packing."

"So I see." The old cowboy leaned against the doorway. "What I can't figure out is why."

"It's time I was moving on."

"Mov—you're leaving?"

He ignored Willie's surprised look and headed for the bathroom to gather his stuff. Toothbrush, toothpaste, shaving cream—he refused to allow his eyes to stray to the shower. Hell, it didn't matter. Every morning and every night, he stood there, icy water raining down his body. He'd hoped it would stop the memory of him and Maggie showering together that night, enveloped in a world of steam, soap suds and sex.

It didn't. Nothing did.

He returned to the main room, not surprised to see the old cowboy still there. "I thought you had something to do in the barn?"

"Seems I've got my work cut out for me right here, dealing with a stubborn jackass." Willie slammed the door shut behind him. "What in hell's bells do you think you're doing?"

"What I have to." He shoved the items in one of his bags, his fingers colliding with the cell phone. He was out of minutes after Bryce's last call yesterday. He'd relayed pretty much the same information Maggie had told him the night they'd shared a beer on the cabin's front porch. Greeley was a weasel of a man, but he wasn't into anything illegal. In fact, he'd backed off lately on bothering Maggie altogether. "Things are running fine here and with those two returning cowboys, you've got plenty of help. You don't need me anymore."

"Bull-hockey."

"This was temporary. I took the job to help G.W. and fill in while Hank healed. Both are doing well. It's time to move on."

Landon was surprised to feel Willie's hand on his shoulder. "You can't outrun it, boy. Take it from someone who knows."

His hands stilled over the bags, and he was glad Willie stood behind him. "I don't know what you're talking about."

"Yes, you do, son. I've been where you are, done what you're doing."

Landon looked up. In the reflection of the dresser's mirror, he watched Willie walk to the kitchen table, and stop, his battered cowboy hat in his hands.

"When I got back from Korea, I walked away from my schooling and a pretty young thing wearing a promise ring. I couldn't get what I'd seen over there out of my head." The natural grittiness of the old man's voice faded to a rough whisper. "The faces of those young boys, their desperate cries for help, the smell of death—whoever said 'war is hell' knew what he was talking about. Living with the hell afterwards…that's the real trick. After all these years, I still sometimes wake up reaching for my medical kit."

Landon dropped his gaze. The bags blurred and he had to swallow hard. "Does it ever go away?"

"Nope. But you find your way. You learn to live with it."

"That's what I'm doing." Landon cleared his throat when his words came out with a rough edge. "Learning to live with it."

"Don't wait too long to get it figured out, boy. I went back East a decade later, but life had moved on without me."

Landon turned around. "You're happy here, aren't you? With your life?"

"Sure am, being a cowboy is the life I was meant to live." Willie slammed his hat back on his head. "But there were times when I'd think about—" The old man rubbed his hand across the gray whiskers on his chin. "Sometimes memories are good friends, and sometimes they'll rub ya raw over what might've been."

"Do me a favor, will you? Hitch the trailer to my truck?" Without waiting for an answer, Landon went back to his packing. Soon, the clomping of boots told him Willie was heading for the door.

"You best not drive out of here without saying goodbye," Willie said. "She deserves that much."

Which *she* was the old man referring to? Nana B.? Anna? Maggie?

All three had found their way into his heart. A heart that didn't have room. All of them, especially Maggie, deserved so much more. He wasn't the man to give it to her. Not now. Not ever.

"How well do you know this new cowboy of yours?"

The coffee mug shook as Maggie handed it to Leeann. She'd been surprised when her friend said she was here on official business. Maggie had ushered her into the house, glad her grandmother and Anna were shopping in Cheyenne.

"Why are you asking?" She busied herself with putting the yellow roses Spence had given her in a glass vase. She cursed her shaking hands and placed the flowers in the center of the kitchen table. "I told you last week at lunch how great he's been around here."

"I know you did." Leann took a seat at the kitchen table. "Right after you told me how he stepped in when Kyle Greeley was giving you a hard time at the fair and how he saved Anna from that wild horse, but that's not what I'm asking. What do you know about his past? Where he came from? Where he worked before showing up in Destiny?"

Maggie grabbed her own coffee mug. "He gave me a list of references."

"Which you never called."

She bit her bottom lip before answering. "How do you know that?"

Leann sighed. "I know you. Despite your jerk of a father and an ex-husband who couldn't keep his pants zipped, you're still the most trusting woman in the county."

Her friend's words stuck hard. "Don't be shy, Lee. Tell me how you really feel."

"I feel like you're being taken for a ride, Maggie. I know things have worsened since Alan took off. Your ongoing war with Greeley over cowboys is the least of it, but you hire this total stranger and allow him to take over the running of the Moon?"

"Hey, I run the Moon."

"You said yourself he's come up with some great ideas—"

"He has, but nothing was put in place without my approval."

"And where do you think he got those great ideas?" Leeann pulled in a deep breath and set the mug on the table. She laid her hand on the folder in front of her. "I've got the official report for the fire here. You're going to need it for your insurance company. There's also a background check on Landon Cartwright."

Maggie set her mug on the table hard. "What?"

"It's standard procedure. We ran it when he and Willie reported their suspicions about Hank's wagon."

"You told me it was an accident."

"It was, but the report on Cartwright was misfiled. I found it today." Leeann opened the folder. "Do you know he's a one-third owner of a ranch in Texas called—"

"Still Waters."

Leeann looked up. "He told you?"

Maggie nodded, her hand gripping the back of the chair. "Yes. He arranged a horse sale to his brother, who runs the ranch."

"And you don't think it strange the man is working a thousand miles away from his home—" she paused to look over the report "—a place five times the size of the Crescent Moon, as a hired hand?"

"He told me—" A loud knocking on the back door interrupted Maggie. She answered it, surprised to see Kyle Greeley and two men standing there. "Kyle, I don't have time for a visit now."

"You better make time. I need to talk to you."

"If this is about my cowboys walking out on you, there's nothing to discuss," Maggie said, fuming. "It's a free country and men can work for whomever they want."

"This isn't about them. It's about you. And Cartwright."

Maggie's hand fell away from the doorjamb. "You, too?"

Kyle stepped inside, pausing to send away his men with a quick jerk of his head before closing the door. "What does that mean?"

"Nothing." She watched Leeann rise from the table. "As you can see I've got company. Can you make this quick?"

Kyle nodded at Leeann. "Deputy Harris."

"Greeley." Her voice held a bitter edge, her mouth pulled into a thin-lipped smile.

Maggie went back to the table, grabbed her mug and tossed its contents into the sink. "What do you want, Kyle?"

"I have some information on Cartwright you need to know."

Maggie crossed her arms over her chest. "I know all I need to." *Or I will once I get my hands on the folder.* What more could they tell her? She already knew the most horrific aspects of Landon's life.

"He's married," Kyle said.

How does he know that? "No, he's not. His wife and daughter died in a fire five years ago."

"A fire he was convicted of setting."

Shock flew through her. She was barely able to control her gasp at the bombshell. It mutated into denial. "No, you're wrong."

Leeann moved to her side. "Maggie—"

Kyle took a step toward her. "I'm not wrong. I'm telling you this because I'm worried, and with the fire—I know you hired him to be spiteful. He's a smooth talker. I was fooled, too, but you need—"

"No," Maggie repeated and backed away from his out-stretched hand. Her mind raced with Landon's words. *His responsibility. His fault.* "I can't—"

"The conviction was manslaughter," Kyle continued. "You don't want his kind around your family. Let me take care of this. I'll get him off your land—"

"Maggie, listen to me." Leeann stepped in front of Kyle, cutting off his words. "It's true, but there's more you need to know—"

"That's all she needs to know," Kyle bellowed. "She needs to throw that felon off her land."

Leeann whirled around, and jabbed at Kyle's chest with her finger. "I think you should leave. You've accomplished what you've set out to do here."

"Hey, I'm trying to help."

"No, you're not," Leeann said. "You want me to make this official, fine. Kyle Greeley, you need to leave this property right now or I'll arrest you for trespassing."

Maggie shook her head and moved away from them. "Both of you get out. This can't be true. It can't be."

"It is."

Her head whipped around. Landon stood there, his black hat cradled in his hands.

"It's true, Maggie. All of it."

Chapter Fifteen

"Leeann, Kyle." Maggie's voice was soft. "I think it's best if you leave now. Don't ask me if I'm sure, because I am."

"I'm not going anywhere," Kyle sputtered.

A heated flash sparked in Landon's eyes, but he didn't look away from her. "Deputy Harris," she began, praying no one noticed the wobble in her voice, "will you please escort Mr. Greeley off my property?"

"Let's go, Kyle," Leeann directed.

Kyle stomped toward the back door, pausing when he neared Landon. "It's all over for you, cowboy."

Landon tightened his grip on his Stetson, but didn't reply.

Leeann gave Kyle a push on his shoulder, forcing him to move. "If you need anything, Maggie, call me. I won't be far away."

Maggie nodded. They walked out the door, leaving her and Landon in the kitchen.

He lied to me. He lied to me. He lied to me.

The words echoed in her head. The room started to spin. She

closed her eyes to get her bearings. Bad idea. She swayed and grabbed for the table.

"Maggie—"

Her eyes flew open. Landon had crossed the room in a heartbeat. Her gaze focused on the tanned, smooth column of his throat revealed by the three open buttons of his shirt.

Why would she notice something so simple at a time like this?

"Don't." She backed away. "Don't touch...I...I need a minute..."

No, she needed more. She needed the truth. And air. And space. The kitchen was too confining. Landon filled it completely with his height, his scent and the memories of shared meals with her family.

Her family. How was she going to explain this to them?

"Come with me." She headed for the back door. Once outside, she didn't stop until she stood in the cool shade of the cottonwood trees. "Now, I think you owe me an explanation."

"What Greeley told you is true," he said. "I was tried and convicted of second-degree manslaughter and second-degree arson."

Her stomach rolled, and she had to swallow back a vile taste in her throat. "What exactly does that mean?"

"The fire was my fault."

Jagged pieces of his past fell into place. "That's why you left home four years ago. You haven't been roaming the country. You went to prison."

Landon nodded.

"But now you're out? Those sound like serious charges. How did you—" Maggie stopped when Willie led G.W. out of the barn and tied him to the end of the horse trailer, hitched to the back of Landon's pickup.

Ohmigod, he's leaving.

She marched to the truck while Willie made a hasty retreat. Landon's duffel bags were inside. She spun around. "It doesn't matter, does it? That I know the truth. You're leaving."

"It's time for me to go. We both knew this was temporary."

"And temporary isn't going to work anymore?"

She threw his words back at him, pain and anguish tearing at her heart. She'd never hurt like this in her life. Neither her father's harsh child rearing nor Alan's leaving cut as deep as this man's words. It'd taken her a long time to come to terms with her father's lack of parenting skills and realize she had to use her childhood as an example of how not to raise Anna. She'd always be grateful for her daughter, but her shock at Alan's departure had over time boiled down to the belief they'd married too young and it was for the best.

This was, too.

It would take a while—who was she kidding, it would take forever—but she would get this man out of her head and out of her heart.

Maggie suppressed the throbbing pain, allowing rage to take its place—rage at her foolishness for letting this man past her defenses. "So, all you did, all that happened here…it doesn't mean anything to you?"

A muscle twitched along Landon's jaw. His hands curled into tight fists as his dark eyes looked at her. "No."

"Get off my land." Her voice was quiet, but held a cold contempt. "Now."

She pushed past him and headed for the barn. She had to get away from here. A hot rush of tears blinded her as she stumbled toward Black Jack's corral. Thankful to find him fully saddled from their earlier workout, she swung open the gate, jumped on his back and took off.

Landon called out her name, but she didn't stop. She didn't want to hear anything else from him. She couldn't watch him drive away.

Landon had to plant his feet in the dirt to keep from going after her. He'd hurt her. Deeply. He wondered if it matched the bottomless ache in his gut. "Don't think about it," he lectured himself. "You're doing what's best. For her, for everyone."

The sound of a vehicle pulling into the driveway caught his attention. He braced himself before turning around. If it was Maggie's deputy friend, he'd assure her he was on his way out. If it was Greeley, he could do the same thing, but it might include a hard right to the arrogant man's jaw.

"Laudsakes," Nana B. called out from the driver's side of Maggie's truck. "You look like you're heading out of town."

"Yes, ma'am, I am."

The smile fell from her face. "You want to tell me what for?"

"It's time I was moving on."

"Does Maggie know?"

"She knows."

A ball of energy leapt over her grandmother and raced to him. Landon dropped to one knee in time for Anna to rush into his arms. "No, Landon, you can't leave," she cried. "We need you here."

"Out of the mouths of babes," Nana B. muttered, stepping from the truck.

Closing his eyes against the powerful longing that surged inside, Landon found himself holding on to Maggie's little girl when he should be letting her go.

He waited for the ache that would compare this little angel to the daughter he'd lost, but it never came. Over the last few weeks, it had slowly ebbed away with each moment spent with Anna. He was dangerously close to letting her, and her mother, inside the hollow remains of his heart.

That couldn't happen.

"Sorry, Little Bit, but I'm needed elsewhere." He set her away from him. The sight of tears on her cheeks made a hard lump form in his chest. "Besides, you've got all the help you need right here. Your mom hired back Spence and Charlie this morning, and Hank is right as rain now."

"But I don't want you to go."

Landon rose, clearing his throat. "Well, darling, sometimes we don't get what we want."

"Sometimes a body is too much a fool to see what's right in front of them."

Landon looked at Maggie's grandmother. "This is for the best, Nana B."

"I can't say I agree." Nana B. handed two bags to her great-granddaughter. "Anna, take these into the house, please. I'll be right behind ya. We've got a truck to empty."

"I'm gonna miss you, Landon." Anna took the bags and headed for the porch stairs, her sneakered feet dragging across the dirt. "Real bad."

The lump in his chest moved to his throat. "You take good care of those kittens."

"I will."

Landon turned away to find Nana B. standing there.

"Well, I thank you for all your hard work. And for the sale of our horses to your brother's ranch." Nana B. smiled then continued. "Yes, Maggie told me about you and Still Waters. I hope between the sale and the fees she's pulling in from Black Jack it's enough to keep Greeley happy."

"What are you talking about?"

"Maggie didn't tell you Greeley took over a board position at the bank?"

Landon shook his head.

Nana B. frowned. "Well, maybe it's not my place to say anything, but hell, I never did learn to hold my tongue. With his position, Greeley has power over the note the bank holds on the ranch. Maggie had to use the land as collateral in order to pay off that good-for-nothing ex-husband of hers."

"She never said anything."

"I understand, but she's been fretting about a final payment—don't you never mind." She waved her words away and grabbed a box from the truck's back seat. "You've got your own plans."

"Need any help with that?" he asked.

"You best head out now you've said your goodbyes." She looked at him. "It will break her heart more, the longer you stick around."

Landon was surprised to see tears in her eyes. He knew Maggie would tell her what she'd learned about him. There'd be no tears then. She'd be happy he was out of her granddaughter's life. "Take care of her, of them."

Nana B. nodded. He leaned inside the truck, pulled out the last half-dozen bags and followed her onto the porch and set the bags inside.

"Thank you, Landon," she said, without looking at him. "Now, shoo."

"Yes, ma'am."

He went to G.W., pausing to take what would be his last look around the Crescent Moon. It was a different place than a month ago. He'd had a hand in the ranch coming back to life, and it was a good thing. He was confident things were moving in the right direction for Maggie and her land.

Greeley notwithstanding. Landon didn't think he could take over the Moon just because he was part of the bank's board of directors. Of course, if Greeley had them in his back pocket—

Knock it off! It doesn't matter. You can't be what Maggie and her family need. Besides, you were told by the boss woman herself to get off her land.

A racing pile of dust coming in from the back pasture caught his eye. Someone was riding fast, too fast. It had to be Maggie. Guess he didn't get out of here quick enough to suit her. He yanked on G.W.'s rope. Ten minutes, fifteen tops. Then he'd be gone.

What the hell?

The horse got closer, its path uneven, as if—dammit!

Fear, harsh and vivid, raced through his veins. He ran to the corral as Black Jack raced by the barn. He stepped in front of the horse and waved his hands in the air. "Whoa, boy, easy there, easy."

The horse reared backward. The sight of the empty saddle sent a riot of panic inside Landon. He forced it back. "Easy, Black Jack, calm down. No one's going to hurt you."

Sweat soaked the animal, and he noticed a trail of dark liquid coming from beneath the saddle. Blood. Black Jack darted past him. Landon lunged for the reins, allowing the horse to drag him toward the corral.

Once the stallion was inside, Landon slammed the gate closed. "Willie! Nana B.!"

Both came running.

"Call the sheriff and the vet." He rushed back to his trailer and easily leapt on G.W.'s bare back. "Maggie took off on Black Jack, but something went wrong. I'm going after her."

"I'll go with ya," the old cowboy said.

"No. Black Jack means everything to Maggie, and he's hurt bad. Take care of the horse. I'll take care of Maggie."

He didn't stick around to see if they'd listened. He didn't have time. Two quick nudges into G.W.'s flank was all the animal needed. The horse took off, and Landon was thankful for the halter and lead rope. They raced off in the direction Black Jack had come.

Where was she? The Crescent Moon had over twenty thousand acres. She could be anywhere. He followed the trail the horse had left, praying the beast hadn't gone off on a wild tear through the countryside. Landon urged G.W. faster, his gaze moving back and forth between the ground and the horizon, praying he'd come across a pissed-off Maggie walking back to the house.

Nothing.

He realized they were heading to the northwest section of the ranch, an area that ran into the foothills of the Laramie Mountains. One of Willie's stories filled his head. How, when

Maggie would run off as a child, she'd always head for the dense, cool forest of the foothills.

Had she gone that way again?

G.W. slowed as the low, scraggy shrubs gave way to towering ponderosa pines and sprawling junipers. Landon checked his watch. Twenty minutes since he'd left the house. Depending on where the sheriff was, it could be another half hour before any help arrived.

He reached for the cell phone in his pocket, then realized he'd left it back in his truck. The walkie-talkie was on the cabin's dresser. Hell, he'd never felt more useless in his life. He had to find her.

G.W. struggled to find solid footing in the soft earth. They made their way up a ragged trail that went to the edge of a ravine, then headed back to where the hills met the flatlands again. The trail wound back to the ravine and away two more times, until they came to the last foothill, the largest so far, with a sharp drop-off at its peak where the ground fell away.

Then he saw it. A straw cowboy hat caught on an outcropping of rocks.

"Maggie!"

He called out again as he slid from G.W.'s back, a sick feeling in his gut as he made his way to the ravine. He flattened his body on the ground, and leaned over the edge. His breath stopped when he spotted Maggie lying motionless ten feet below on a ledge.

"Maggie!" He forced his words from his throat. "Maggie, honey, can you hear me? Maggie?"

Leaving his hat next to hers, he slid over the edge, making his way down the serrated cliff, mindless of the rocks cutting into his skin. Seconds later, he was next to her. He gently turned her face to him and leaned close. Relief filled him as the gentle rush of her breath caressed his cheek.

"Maggie, honey, it's going to be okay. I'm here." Landon

spoke softly, his hands checking her arms and legs. "Come on, honey, please wake up."

His fingers brushed her hair off her face then carefully circled her head, encountering a large, wet bump. He pulled back, his hand tangled in blond hair and blood.

Oh, God.

He looked up and let out a sharp whistle. He could hear G.W. pawing at the ground in response. "Home," he ordered his horse, and let loose a series of short, shrill blasts. "Home."

After a quick prayer his buddy would both remember the old trick and consider the Moon's barn home, Landon listened as G.W. took off. They had to be out looking for them by now; he hoped they'd find his horse.

He returned his attention to Maggie. The bandanna she usually wore at her wrist was gone. Then he remembered the folded cotton and lace handkerchief in his pocket. The same one Maggie had offered to him the first night they met. He'd meant to return it earlier when he'd gone to the kitchen to tell her goodbye.

"Baby, wake up and show me those pretty green eyes." He pulled the pale blue scrap of cloth from his pocket and held it against her head. "Get angry I'm here, I followed you, anything."

He continued to lean over her, shielding her from the hot sun. "You've got to wake up, Maggie. Your ranch and family can't survive without you. Things are heading in the right direction now. Your cowboys are coming back and you'll have Black Jack eating out of your hand no matter what happened today. All you needed was new ideas and some help…"

The threat of tears choked off his words, but he pushed through them. "You're the heart and soul of the Moon. This land would be nothing without you."

I would be nothing.

It was true. The coincidence of their meeting, of her needing help and his needing to take care of his horse wasn't an accident or a twist of fate. Their meeting had led to him feeling alive, truly alive for the first time in years. The fire at Still Waters had taken more than his family. It had killed his spirit, hardened his heart and blackened his soul. He'd ceased to do more than exist.

Until this woman. Until she, her crazy family and her run-down ranch had found a way to bring him back to life.

"But I can't…no matter how much I want—" He dropped his brow to her forehead. "I can't let myself love you…"

The thunder of hoofs and people calling out filled the air. Landon jerked upright. "Hey! We're here! Down here!"

Moments later three heads peered over the edge of the ravine. Hank, Willie and Sheriff Steele.

"Damn, how is she?" the lawman barked.

"Unconscious, but no broken bones, I think," Landon said. "She's got a good-sized lump on her head, and it's bleeding. We've got to get her out of here."

"I'll get my EMTs—"

"There's not enough room for all of us down here."

"There will be when you come up."

"Forget it. I'm not going anywhere. There's enough room for one more person. Send him down. We'll strap her in and you can pull her up."

The sheriff stared at him. Landon had no idea what he was thinking, but he disappeared and began shouting out orders. A few minutes later, a rope came over the side, then a pair of black boots. Landon shielded Maggie with his body as the medical technician with a rescue basket scrambled to join them.

They got Maggie secure in the basket and latched to the ropes. Both held the basket steady as she was lifted. Landon kept his hands on her as long as he could, then let go.

The rope came back and the technician climbed up, then Landon. At the top, a large hand stretched over the edge. He grabbed it and the sheriff pulled him up. "Thanks," Landon said.

Steele nodded in reply. "They're stabilizing her. How long has she been unconscious?"

"I don't know." Landon tried to watch the EMTs work, but he couldn't see much with Willie and Hank hovering over Maggie. "Forty-five minutes? Maybe an hour. How'd you find us?"

The sheriff motioned to G.W., who stood nearby with the other horses. "Willie saw your palomino—"

"Okay, we're ready to move her." The technicians moved to either side of the basket. "We need to carry her to the flats, then get her to the hospital. I don't think anything's broken, but the abrasion on her head and being unconscious—"

A low moan sounded and everyone focused on Maggie. Landon couldn't stop himself from moving closer. Willie knelt on one side, Hank on the other. He had to be content with leaning over Willie's shoulder.

"Come on, Maggie," the technician cajoled as he took her hand. "Wake up, cowgirl."

Landon bit back the same words as Maggie's eyes fluttered and she slowly opened them.

"What—what's going on?" she asked.

"Easy there." The technician laid a hand on her shoulder. "You took quite a tumble. Can you tell me your name?"

"Ronny, it's me, Maggie," she mumbled, then she said more clearly, "I gave you your first black eye during a game of spin-the-bottle back in the fourth grade."

The technician smiled. "You're right, you did. I think you're going to be just fine."

Relief rushed over Landon as Maggie's beautiful green eyes looked at each man. When she got to him, they widened in shock. "What are you doing—" she tried to lift her head. "I told you…to leave."

"You rest." Ronny covered her with a soft blanket. "We're going to get you to the hospital."

"We'll help," Willie and Hank said in unison.

Pain lanced through Landon when Maggie closed her eyes and turned away.

"You better stay with me," the sheriff said to him. "We need to talk."

"About what?"

Steele motioned for Landon, Willie and Hank to move away from Maggie and the medical technicians. "Kali radioed to say a chunk of metal was found embedded in Black Jack's backside. It was stuck beneath the saddle. As long as Maggie leaned forward, the animal was okay. As soon as she sat back—"

"It cut into the horse." Fury built inside Landon. "And you think I did this?"

Both Willie and Hank protested, but the sheriff held up a hand. "I need to talk to everyone connected to the ranch." He looked at Landon. "Starting with you."

Hank and Willie left to help with Maggie. Forced to do nothing as they carried her away, Landon punched out deep breaths, squashing his desire to jump on G.W. and race after them. Once they were out of sight, he turned and found the sheriff holding out Landon's battered Stetson. He took it and placed it on his head, shocked to see the lawman's hand extended in greeting.

"Gage Steele. Sheriff," he said.

Landon took the hand. "Landon Cartwright. Ex-con."

They let go, and the sheriff swung onto a big black gelding, reaching for the reins of Hank's horse. "I know who you are, Mr. Cartwright. I read the report. An overturned conviction means you're a good man who got a raw deal. My sympathies for your family."

Landon ducked his head to hide his surprise and climbed onto G.W., taking control of Willie's mustang.

"So, you have any idea of how the metal got under the horse's saddle?" asked the sheriff.

Landon tipped up the brim of his hat and looked him in the eye. "What would you do if I said to ask Kyle Greeley?"

Chapter Sixteen

I can't let myself love you.

Landon's whispered declaration came back to Maggie during her overnight stay at the hospital. The words woke her from a restless sleep, as if he'd spoken them right there instead of hours earlier. Now home and tucked in her own bed under Nana B.'s care, she couldn't get his words from her head.

Maggie gingerly touched the bandage that covered the sutures.

She closed her eyes. The events were a bit fuzzy, but she recalled being upset and taking off on Black Jack. She'd pushed the animal into a fast run and it was only when they reached the foothills that she sat back full in the saddle. The next thing she remembered was the poor animal's pain-filled squeal and being thrown from the saddle. Then the sound of Landon's voice.

"Hey there, you up for company?"

Maggie's eyes flew open. She pushed herself up against her pillows and smiled. A balloon bouquet filled the doorway, almost obliterating Racy behind the array of color. "You're a nut."

Racy pushed the balloons into the room. "Takes one to know one." She released the ribbons and they floated upwards, then she dragged a wicker chair to the bed. "See, they made you smile."

Maggie looked from the balloons against the ceiling to her friend. "Thanks. Anna will love them."

Racy sat, tucking one jean-clad leg beneath her. "So, how are you doing? Really?"

"I'm fine. A cut on the back of my head and some bumps and bruises. Thank goodness Black Jack is going to be okay, too. If we could only find out who tried to hurt him."

"I bet you talked to Kali as soon as you got home."

"Being the wonderful vet she is, she didn't balk when I called last night from my hospital bed," Maggie said. "Then I called Tucker Hargrove."

"Yeah? How'd the two-time Oscar-winner react to the news about his daughter's prized horse?"

"He didn't blame me," Maggie said, sighing, "and he wants me to continue working with Black Jack once he's healed."

"I think the man needs to worry more about his daughter's behavior," Racy huffed, tossing a long curly strand of hair over her shoulder. "Hailey Hargrove spends more time in the tabloids than on movie sets."

"She's eighteen. I remember a couple teenagers who weren't above having a good time now and then."

"Oh, please. Bonfires at the lake and a few cases of beer are small potatoes compared to what that young lady has done."

"Speaking of daughters…" Maggie's smile expanded when her daughter peeked into the room. "Here's my favorite."

Anna smiled. "That's 'cause you've only got one." Her eyes grew wide when she noticed the balloons. "Golly! Where'd they come from?"

"The balloon fairy." Racy grinned.

Giggling, Anna came in and raised her hands, brushing her fingertips through the ribbon tails of the balloons. "I like the pink ones."

"You can take a few and put them in your room after dinner," Maggie said.

"Okay. Nana said to tell you everyone's ready to eat."

Maggie's stomach tightened to a hard knot. "Everyone?"

"Yep. Nana's done cooking, Hank set the table and Willie, Spence, Charlie and Landon are washing up."

"Ah, sweetie, I'm feeling a bit tired. Can you please ask Nana to fix me a tray and I'll eat in here? Racy, too."

"Okay."

Anna skipped from the room, closing the door behind her. Maggie looked at her friend and saw the suspicion in her eyes. "Don't ask, Rac."

"You're avoiding him?"

"Yes."

"At least you aren't denying it."

Maggie sighed, pleating the sheets with her fingers. "I don't understand why he's still here."

"Maybe for the same reason he was outside your hospital room all night."

Maggie's eyes widened. "What?"

"I stopped by when I got off work. He was there."

"It must have been after two o'clock in the morning."

Racy shrugged. "I snuck in. Anyway, I found his six-foot-plus frame propped up in one of those waiting-room chairs."

Landon at the hospital? All night? No one had told her.

Her mind reeled. It was too much.

Discovering he'd spent time in prison, that she and her family meant nothing to him, that making love meant nothing. But then he'd saved her, said he couldn't fall in love with her, stayed at the hospital all night...

Fresh pain stabbed at her heart.

"Maggie." Racy took her hand. "What is it?"

"Noth—nothing." She shook her head. "I'm fine."

"You want to tell me what's going on between you and your cowboy?" Racy sat back in the chair. "We haven't talked in a while, but I can hear something in your voice whenever you say his name."

She closed her eyes against her friend's inquisitive stare. "There's nothing between me and Landon…anymore. It doesn't matter. It's over."

"Is that the reason he's got a horse trailer attached to his truck?"

Maggie's eyes shot to her friend. "You don't miss much." Then she sighed. "I fired him and he should already be gone, except for—"

"He saved your life?" Racy cut her off. "And what do you mean you fired him? Why?"

A knock at the door saved Maggie from answering. "Come in."

Her grandmother opened the door. "I thought you'd like to know the sheriff and Leeann are here."

"Well, that's my cue. I'm outta here." Racy grabbed her bag and stood.

"Honey, I'm afraid you can't," Nana B. said. "The sheriff pulled in right behind you, blocked your car."

Racy let out an exasperated breath. "Of course he did! You have room to park twenty vehicles and where does he put his Jeep? Right on my ass!"

Nana B. smiled, then became serious. "Maggie, something tells me this isn't a social call."

"You're probably right." She kicked away the blankets. They had to be here because of Black Jack.

"Are you feeling well enough to get out of bed?" Racy handed her a pair of jeans and a shirt. "A minute ago you were determined to stay there."

Maggie ignored her and shimmied off her pajama bottoms.

"You know the boys will insist on hearing what the sheriff has to say."

Maggie's fingers faltered on the zipper of her jeans. Her grandmother was including Landon when she said *boys*.

She breathed deeply, then released it, doing little to settle the butterflies in her stomach. "They have a right to know what's going on, but if you could keep Anna distracted—"

"Don't you worry, she and I will be in the garden picking veggies. But I expect a full report later."

Maggie agreed and slipped on a pair of sneakers. She glanced at the mirror. It was useless to try to do anything with her hair. Not with the large compress and bandage wrapped around her head.

You worried about impressing someone?

Pushing aside the thought, she headed for the kitchen with Racy at her heels. They stepped into the sunny room as Hank opened the back door for Gage and Leeann. She tried to keep her gaze away from Landon, but it was impossible.

Dressed from head to toe in black, he stood in the corner closest to the back door, his attention on Gage. As if he knew she was watching, he turned and locked eyes with her. Spence broke the spell by stepping in front of him to join Charlie at the table.

"So, did you smell Nana B.'s steak sandwiches all the way into town?" Maggie asked, thankful her voice came out unruffled. "Or is this an official visit?"

"It's official." Gage removed his hat. He took a moment to look over the crowded room. Maggie noted his gaze lingered a second longer on Racy, who was leaning against the counter. "If you prefer, we can talk in private."

Maggie moved to the table and rested her hands on the back of a chair. "If this has to do with Black Jack then please go ahead. We're all family—" Her hands tightened on the wood, as this time she succeeded in not looking at Landon. "We're all in this together."

"Maggie, maybe you should sit," Leeann said.

"Why?" The faint pain in her head took a sharp jump. "Did something happen to Black Jack?"

"No." Her friend rushed to her. "You look like someone—"

"Who fell over the side of a cliff and cracked her head open on a rock?" Maggie interrupted. "I know. Now, tell me what's going on."

Leeann glanced at Gage, who nodded. She looked back at Maggie. "We arrested Steve Walker and Butch Dickens a couple hours ago."

Greeley's foremen. "Why?"

Gage stepped forward. "It started with what Spence and Charlie told me—"

"Hey, we didn't know anything about this," Charlie protested.

Spence nodded in agreement. "Mr. Greeley made it no secret he wanted the Crescent Moon, and he boasted how he had the means to get it. We never figured he was doing more than hiring cowboys away from you."

"It's all right," Maggie said. "I believe you."

"Like I was saying," Gage continued, "I spoke to Spence and Charlie after I talked with Landon."

"Landon?" Unable to stop her gaze from flying across the room, Maggie noted his clenched jaw and the tight press of his mouth. His dark eyes revealed nothing as they fixed on her.

Gage cleared his throat. Maggie looked back at him. "Ah, you said you talked to Landon?"

"I talked with everyone connected with the Crescent Moon, and then I spoke with Kali Watson. She brought me the piece of metal she'd taken out of Black Jack."

"What was it?" Maggie asked.

"A rowel from a handmade set of spurs. We put out a few calls and did some checking on the Internet. We found a designer who'd been in town for the Fourth of July carnival and matched the style to him. He said he only sold three sets while here. Two were to locals and one to a cowboy who was passing through."

Gage slapped his hat against his thigh and continued. "One of them was Butch Dickens. As soon as I showed Dickens the rowel, he offered to talk if we cut him a deal. He confessed he and Steve have been causing trouble around here, everything from cutting your fence line to messing with Black Jack. They claimed not to have had anything to do with your tool shed, that the fire and Hank's wagon wheel giving way were just accidents that worked in Greeley's favor. But we may reopen our investigation of those incidents."

A chorus of gruff, hushed curses filled the air. The strength left Maggie's legs and she dropped into the chair. "Why would he tell you all that?"

"Because everything they did was on orders from Kyle Greeley. We've just arrested him. He's in custody on a variety of charges from harassment to animal cruelty. The county district attorney is still considering attempted murder."

Disbelief filled Maggie. Kyle had made it no secret he wanted her land, but to go this far? The disbelief turned to guilt. She should've realized the events happening around the Moon, events she'd chalked up to bad luck, were actually part of something more sinister.

She closed her eyes, and felt Leeann grabbing one hand. Seconds later, Racy gripped the other. Pulling in a deep breath, she returned their touch with a quick squeeze. "I'm— it's okay. I'm okay."

Willing back the tears, she opened her eyes. "Kyle did all this because he wants my land that badly?"

"He didn't say anything, just demanded his lawyer," Leeann said. "We need to get an official statement about what's happened between the two of you."

Maggie nodded. The effects of her inner turmoil slowly ebbed away. It was going to be all right now. With the ranch, anyway. For the first time in a long while, relief filled her. She still owed the bank, but she was sure she could work out something. She had her contract to work with Black Jack and the ranch was running better than it had in years.

Thanks to Landon.

Her gaze roamed to the men who worked for her, purposely avoiding Landon's tall frame at the door. "I'm sorry you all had to go through this. I should've known something—someone was doing—"

"Magpie, there's no way you could've known," Hank assured her. "None of us realized the depth of Greeley's greed. We're sorry we didn't push the issue and get the law involved before you were hurt."

Tears bit at the back of Maggie's eyes, but she blinked them away.

"Seems to me we're letting a perfectly good meal go to waste," Willie chimed in. "Let's chow!"

Maggie shot Willie a grateful look, then insisted Gage and Leeann join them. Hank called in Nana B. and Anna from the garden. Racy went to work with her usual efficiency and served a platter of sandwiches and ice tea for everyone.

Leeann leaned in. "Hey, Maggie, you got a second?"

Maggie nodded and followed her into the living room.

"I didn't want to say anything in front of the crowd, because I don't know what you've told them, but I'm glad Landon was here for you yesterday. After Greeley showed up spouting about Landon's past, I think he was planning to use the man's history against him. To try to get everyone to believe Landon was connected to what happened to you. I think you did the right thing keeping him around."

A dull ache settled in Maggie's chest. Yes, things were looking up for her. Except where he was concerned.

"Leeann, I fired him."

"What?"

"The only reason Landon is here is because Black Jack came back to the barn before he left."

"You mean you fired him after he told you about his conviction being—" Leeann paused "—wait, he didn't tell you, did he?"

"Tell me what?"

"Damn! I swear, when it comes to men and secrets—" Leafing through the folder in her hand, Leeann pulled out a sheet of paper. "Read this. You deserve to know the whole truth about Landon Cartwright."

He forced himself to keep walking toward his truck when all he wanted to do was march right back into the house.

Maggie's house.

It'd taken every ounce of strength not to react when the sheriff had told them what had happened over the last twenty or so hours. He'd wanted to push his way past her family and friends, pull her into his arms and make sure she was okay.

But he couldn't. He didn't have any right. She'd be fine now that Greeley's plan was stopped and the man was behind bars. She had everything and everyone she needed right inside her kitchen.

He whistled softly and G.W. came to the corral's edge. The horse waited patiently as Landon opened the gate and led him to the trailer. It took a firm nudge and a verbal command to get the animal inside. He tossed his head and neighed sharply, telling Landon what he thought of the idea.

"Yeah, pal, I hate leaving, too, but it's time for us to be going." Landon closed the trailer, slapping the heated metal sides as he headed back toward the truck's cab. "Past time."

"Without saying goodbye?"

Landon's hand froze on the door handle for a moment, letting the light breeze carry her words and her clean, sweet scent to him. Then he grabbed the handle in a tight grip and opened the door.

Settling himself behind the wheel, he pulled the door shut with a hard tug. "Seeing how you fired me yesterday, not once but twice, I thought it best to get on my way."

She moved to the side of his truck, and thrust a sheet of paper through the open window. "It doesn't matter I know the truth?"

The paper shook so hard, he could barely make out the Texas state seal on the letterhead.

Ah, hell.

He reached for it, but she yanked it back. "How can you leave with me thinking what you said was true?"

"Because it is true." He tightened his grip on the steering wheel. "It doesn't matter what some judge determined. My wife and child are dead, and it's my fault."

"It's not your fault," Maggie cried. "You can't shoulder the blame for a stupid, tragic accident. It never should've happened, but it did, and you suffered a loss no one should have to endure."

"It was my job to keep them safe." Ignoring the need to look at her one last time, Landon forced himself to stare straight ahead. "I failed them. To be responsible again for someone else…I can't do it."

"You can't live in the past. Do you think your wife or daughter would want you torturing yourself this way?"

Landon swallowed hard, but didn't speak.

"Landon—"

"You're going to be okay, Maggie," he said, feeing as if he had to push the words from his mouth. Jamming the keys into the ignition, he gunned the engine to life. "The ranch is safe, and you've got plenty of help to keep things running smoothly. There's nothing more I can do for you."

"You can stay."

Her soft plea floated into the interior of the truck and branded him deeply. His heart pounded unsteadily. The flicker of desire to stick around flared to life again, but he pushed it back. He was doing what was best.

For everyone.

"I can't."

He slowly released the brake, and the truck inched forward. Maggie backed away. He opened his eyes and glanced in the side mirror, determined to look just long enough to make sure she was a safe distance from the vehicle.

The sight of her standing there, arms wrapped around her middle, made it almost impossible to look away.

Slowly she faded into the distance and he lost sight of her completely.

Chapter Seventeen

The crowd gathered in Maggie's backyard raised their voices in unison as they sang "Happy Birthday" to Nana B. Blinking back tears, Maggie watched Anna help her grandmother blow out the candles on her cake. All forty of them. Actually, there were two cakes, thanks to the large crowd of neighbors and friends.

Anna had wanted a candle for every year of her great-grandmother's life, but Nana B. had convinced her one candle for every two years would be sufficient. Curly puffs of smoke lingered over the cakes as Maggie moved them to a side table to cut them up. The sound of a fiddle and guitar tuning told her the festivities would be going on long after sunset.

She wouldn't get much sleep, but why should tonight be different than any other night since…

"Knock it off," she lectured herself. "You know what you have to do. And in two days you're going to do it."

"It's about time."

Maggie turned to find Willie standing there. "What did you say?"

"This place hasn't been the same since he scattered to the wind. It's time you did something about your cowboy."

"He's not my cowboy." Maggie stared at the cakes.

She didn't have to say his name aloud. They both knew whom they were talking about, and Willie was right. Landon's leaving had created an emptiness at the ranch. At first, she'd been angry at his unwillingness to stick around. Then she realized she'd never given him a reason to stay.

"At least not yet," she continued. "But I'm taking those horses to the Still Waters Ranch at the end of the week."

"Don't come back empty-handed."

"Empty-hearted is more like it." The knife stilled over the white frosting as fresh tears filled her eyes. Maggie brushed them away with her free hand. "I was such a fool, Willie."

"Don't be so hard on yourself, darling. That man is carrying a lot of baggage, and he's got to get it packed and stored away. Else he'll never be any good to anyone, least of all you or Anna."

"I never should have let him leave without telling him how I felt."

"You said yourself you weren't sure what was thumping around in your heart until a little while ago. Maybe he needs more time."

"Well, he's got as long as it takes me to drive to Texas." And she had as long as that to figure out exactly what she was going to say. Maggie looked at the cakes. "Now, I trust you to behave while I get the ice cream."

"Me?"

Maggie laughed at the innocent look on the old man's face. She knew as soon as her back was turned, he'd cut himself a big slice. Heading inside, she yanked open the freezer and took out several cartons of ice cream.

She shoved the door closed and caught sight of the notice

held to the fridge with a homemade magnet. In three weeks, she'd give a formal deposition against Kyle Greeley.

The man was out of jail, back on the Triple G, and keeping a low profile. The biggest shock of all was who'd bailed him out. Mick Lofton, a former rodeo star and another son of Richard Greeley's no one knew about, appeared a week after Kyle's arrest. Mick was now officially in charge of the Triple G Ranch and all of its holdings.

The deep rumble of a truck engine had her walking to the kitchen counter and peeking out the window. She froze.

A late-model, shiny black truck with a dual horse trailer pulled to a stop in the crowded drive. Her breath caught. It couldn't be Kyle. He wouldn't dare show his face here. But who—

The driver's side door opened and the setting sun danced off a black Stetson. Shocked, she watched the tall cowboy come around the front of the truck. Dark slacks and polished cowboy boots emphasized long legs. A white dress shirt drew attention to wide shoulders, while the rolled-back cuffs revealed tanned forearms.

Landon.

He'd come back.

Anna ran across the yard and flew into his arms when he crouched to one knee and held her close. They spoke for a few moments, before he gave a gentle tug on one of her braids and rose. The crowd parted as he headed toward her grandmother.

Maggie walked to the screen door, and pushed it open with her hip to see Landon present a gift to Nana B. Her grandmother didn't look at it, instead asking a question Maggie couldn't hear. Whatever he said had her grandmother beaming. Then Willie and Hank joined them and she lost sight of him in the crowd.

Maggie hurried down the steps. She dumped the ice cream on the table and wrapped her arms around herself. Frantically rubbing her skin, she tried to rid the chill seeping to her bones.

No, this wasn't right. She wasn't ready.

She wanted to be the one to surprise him. To catch him off guard when she arrived at his ranch. To blurt out what was in her heart before he had a chance to shut down and send her away.

Grabbing an ice cream scoop, she dug into the closest half gallon and started scooping it into bowls. She made quick work of one container, making a mess in the process. She raised a hand to her mouth and licked the vanilla ice cream from her fingers.

"Need any help?"

Maggie spun around. Landon stood in front of her. His gaze moved slowly from her head to her sandaled feet, igniting a fire inside that effectively erased the coldness. She allowed herself to do the same to him. He'd removed his hat and needed a haircut. Deep, tired lines were etched around his eyes.

He looked perfect.

"What are you doing here?"

A grin tugged his mouth as he nodded toward the crowd. "I wanted to bring your grandmother a birthday gift."

Maggie looked at Nana B. prancing around the yard, lifting her white eyelet skirt to show off her present. "Cowboy boots?"

He looked at her, smile wider now. "I'll have you know those are white quill ostrich and purple alligator-skin boots. I brought a pair for each of the men, too, but they're not purple."

"So, you thought you'd stop by and drop off some gifts?" Maggie heard the anger in her voice. Maybe she hadn't gotten over him walking away. "You think it fixes everything? Makes everything better?"

The smile left his face as his dark eyes stared at her. "No."

"Damn right, no. Why are you—"

Excited squeals from the driveway cut off Maggie's words. She watched her daughter dance around the trailer attached to Landon's truck. Willie slowly led a young, chocolate-brown horse down the back gate.

"Her name is Sunshine and she's the sweetest, most gentle filly a young girl could want." Landon leaned forward, his whispered words caressing her ear. "My brother's been working with her for a month now, but I'm sure you can perform the same magic on her as you did with Black Jack."

He took her arm and turned her to face him. "And with me."

"I—" Maggie struggled to find her voice, lost in the warmth of his hands. "I didn't do anything—"

"Mama! Mama!" Anna raced around the end of the table. "Did you see her? Did you? Her name is Sunshine and she's mine. All mine!"

"I saw her, honey." Maggie pulled from Landon's touch to stroke her daughter's hair. "She's a beauty, and I think you owe someone a thank you."

Anna twirled toward Landon with her arms raised. He put his Stetson back on his head and lifted her. She wrapped her arms around his neck. "Thank you so much, Landon. This is better than the Easter Bunny, my birthday and Christmas combined."

The sight of Landon closing his eyes as he returned her daughter's hug had Maggie pressing trembling fingers to her lips. He had to be thinking about his own little girl, and that he'd never be able to hold her like this. She waited for the pain and anguish to cross his features, but today there was only peace.

"You know, you're lucky you came today." Anna leaned back to look at his face. "Another couple of days and you would've missed my mom."

"Oh, really?" Landon perched Anna on his hip but stared at Maggie. "And where was your mom going?"

"Texas," Anna chirped. "She was taking the horses with her, but Nana B. said she was delivering something more important. Her heart."

Surprise flashed in his dark eyes. "Is that so?"

"Did you bring a gift for my mom, too?"

"Anna!" A fiery blush crept over Maggie's cheeks, both at her daughter's question and what she'd revealed to Landon. "You don't ask something—"

"I sure did." Landon stuck his hand in his pocket and pulled out a black velvet box.

"Wow." Anna reached for it. "Can I see it?"

Landon closed his fingers around the gift. "How about I show it to your mom first? If she likes it, she can show you."

Anna's brow furrowed for a moment. "I guess so. Then can we have cake and ice cream?"

A hysterical laugh at her daughter's words bubbled inside Maggie's throat. It matched the dizzying current that raced through her the moment she saw the small box in his hand.

"I don't think the ice cream is going to wait, Little Bit." Hank appeared and Anna went willingly to him. Spence and Charlie were right behind him. "We'll take over, Magpie. Why don't you two find a quiet place to talk?"

Before she could respond, Landon grabbed her hand and pulled her toward the back steps. He marched across the covered porch to the front of the house, not stopping until they reached the hanging porch swing.

Another one of Landon's projects, Maggie thought, as the noise from the party faded to a muted resonance. She looked at the faded patchwork quilt where she'd sat many nights over the last month reliving every moment, every emotion, and every memory of this man.

And now, he was here.

"I'm not trying to buy my way back into your life, Maggie."

She knew he wasn't. Why had she said those things?

He released her hand. Maggie could do nothing but drop into the softness of the swing.

"Leaving here, leaving you was the hardest thing I've ever done." He paced back and forth in front of her. "I thought I was doing the right thing, but I wasn't home more than two weeks when I realized—"

"You went home?"

Landon stopped, yanked off his hat and tunneled his

fingers through his too-long hair. "Yeah, I went home. Not right away. I stubbornly held on to the things I'd been telling myself for years. But at the oddest times, in the smallest moments, your memory would come to me. You made me realize I wasn't doing the right thing—I was running from the past. My past. I needed to come to terms with that part of my life, and put it to rest before I could think about moving on."

She tried not to stare at the box clenched his fingers. "Are you ready to move on now?"

"Yes."

He dropped beside her, controlling the swing's movement with his powerful legs. Tossing his hat down, he stretched one arm across the back of the swing, and leaned in close. "I used to dream about the night my daughter died. I could hear my wife saying something, but it was never clear to me. When I got back to Still Waters, the nightmare came back, night after night, but instead of fighting it off, I lived it again. Listened to her words…she was blaming herself."

"Oh, Landon."

He pressed his finger gently beneath her chin until she looked into his eyes. "But she was wrong. I was, too. I know that now, and I know I hurt you when I left. I'm sorry. I'll never do it again. I love you, and I want you in my life forever."

He released her and opened the jewelry case. Maggie gasped. Nestled on a cushion of white satin sat a trio of emerald-cut diamonds in a platinum setting.

"Marry me."

Her gaze flew from the ring to Landon. Her girlish heart had leapt at the sight of the box, but she'd never expected this. "But what about your ranch in Texas?"

"My brother is running it, and he's got more help than he knows what to do with." He moved his arm around her back and pulled her closer.

"I want to be here at the Moon with you. I know what this land means to you, the connection it gives to your past and future. I want to share that connection. That future. Maggie, please say you'll marry me."

"Landon, I come with a ready-made family. I don't know how you feel about having more children, but I've always dreamed of—"

"I love Anna and the rest of your family. And I'll always have a place in my heart for Sara." Landon placed his lips at her temple, leaving a gentle kiss. "But I want more kids, plenty of brothers and sisters for Anna, as long as you're their mother. Marry me."

This was the moment. Now or never. She didn't have time to prepare a speech of what was in her heart, her soul. When it came to this man, she wanted him in her life, in all their lives. Nothing else mattered.

"Yes."

He captured her answer with a kiss that seemed to go on forever. Finally he pulled back, took her left hand and slid the ring onto her finger. "You know, one thing would make this moment perfect."

Maggie didn't try to stop her tears this time. "What?"

He raised her hand to his mouth and softly pressed his lips to it. "You could tell me you love me, too."

She cradled his face in her hands and looked into the eyes of the man who would work beside her, love her and support her—all her life. The right kind of man for her. "Landon Cartwright, I love you more than words can possibly say, and I'm going to spend the rest of my life showing you how much."

His smile was deliberate and sensuous as he wiped away her tears. "Starting right now?"

She crawled into his lap and wound her arms around his neck. "Well, after our guests leave, and we convince Anna she can't sleep in the barn with Sunshine, and clean up after the party and—"

Landon pulled her tight, pressing their bodies together. Any thought in her head flew away.

"Sounds like a plan, Miss Maggie. Count me in. Forever."

* * * * *

*Celebrate 60 years of pure reading
pleasure with Harlequin®!*

*Harlequin Presents® is proud to introduce
its gripping new miniseries,*
THE ROYAL HOUSE OF KAREDES.
*An exquisite coronation diamond, split as a symbol of a
warring royal family's feud, is missing! But whoever reunites
the diamond halves will rule all....*

*Welcome to eight brand-new titles that unfold to reveal the
stories of kings and queens, princes and princesses torn
apart by pride and power, but finally reunited by love.*

*Step into the world of Karedes with
BILLIONAIRE PRINCE, PREGNANT MISTRESS.
Available July 2009 from Harlequin Presents®.*

ALEXANDROS KAREDES, SNOW DUSTING the shoulders of his leather jacket and glittering like jewels in his dark hair, stood at the door. Maria felt the blood drain from her head.

"Good evening, Ms. Santos."

His voice was as she remembered it. Deep. Husky. Perfect English, but with the faintest hint of a Greek accent. And cold, as cold as it had been that awful morning she would never forget, when he'd accused her of horrible things, called her terrible names....

"Aren't you going to ask me in?"

She fought for composure. Last time they'd faced each other, they'd been on his turf. Now they were on hers. She was in command here, and that meant everything.

"There's a sign on the door downstairs," she said, her tone every bit as frigid as his. "It says, 'No soliciting or vagrants.'"

His lips drew back in a wolfish grin. "Very amusing."

"What do you want, Prince Alexandros?"

A tight smile eased across his mouth and it killed her that even now, knowing he was a vicious, arrogant man, she couldn't help but notice what a handsome mouth it was. Chiseled. Generous. Beautiful, like the rest of him, which made him living proof that beauty could, indeed, be only skin deep.

"Such formality, Maria. You were hardly so proper the last time we were together."

She knew his choice of words was deliberate. She felt her face heat; she couldn't help that but she damned well didn't have to let him lure her into a verbal sparring match.

"I'll ask you once more, your highness. What do you want?"

"Ask me in and I'll tell you."

"I have no intention of asking you in. Tell me why you're here or don't. It's your choice, just as it will be my choice to shut the door in your face."

He laughed. It infuriated her but she could hardly blame him. He was tall—six-two, six-three—and though he stood with one shoulder leaning against the door frame, hands tucked casually into the pockets of the jacket, his pose was deceptive. He was strong, with the leanly muscled body of a well-trained athlete.

She remembered his body with painful clarity. The feel of him under her hands. The power of him moving over her. The taste of him on her tongue.

Suddenly, he straightened, his laughter gone. "I have not come this distance to stand in your doorway," he said coldly, "and I am not going to leave until I am ready to do so. I suggest you stand aside and stop behaving like a petulant child."

A petulant child? Was that what he thought? This man who had spent hours making love to her and had then accused her of—of trading her body for profit?

Except it had not been love, it had been sex. And the sooner she got rid of him, the better.

She let go of the doorknob and stepped aside. "You have five minutes."

He strolled past her, bringing cold air and the scent of the night with him. She swung toward him, arms folded. He reached past her, pushed the door closed, then folded his arms, too. She wanted to open the door again but she'd be damned if she was going to get into a who's-in-charge-here argument with him. She was in charge, and he would surely see a tussle over the ground rules as a sign of weakness.

Instead, she looked past him at the big clock above her work table.

"Ten seconds gone," she said briskly. "You're wasting time, your highness."

"What I have to say will take longer than five minutes."

"Then you'll just have to learn to economize. More than five minutes, I'll call the police."

Instantly, his hand was wrapped around her wrist. He tugged her toward him, his dark-chocolate eyes almost black with anger.

"You do that and I'll tell every tabloid shark I can contact about how Maria Santos tried to buy a five-hundred-thousand-dollar commission by seducing a prince." He smiled thinly. "They'll lap it up."

* * * * *

What will it take for this billionaire prince to realize
he's falling in love with his mistress…?
Look for
BILLIONAIRE PRINCE, PREGNANT MISTRESS
by Sandra Marton.
Available July 2009 from Harlequin Presents®.

We'll be spotlighting a different series every month throughout 2009 to celebrate our 60th anniversary.

Look for Harlequin® Presents in July!

TWO CROWNS, TWO ISLANDS, ONE LEGACY
A royal family, torn apart by pride and its lust for power, reunited by purity and passion

Step into the world of Karedes beginning this July with

BILLIONAIRE PRINCE, PREGNANT MISTRESS
by
Sandra Marton

Eight volumes to collect and treasure!

You're invited to join our Tell Harlequin Reader Panel!

By joining our new reader panel you will:

- Receive Harlequin® books—they are FREE and yours to keep with no obligation to purchase anything!
- Participate in fun online surveys
- Exchange opinions and ideas with women just like you
- Have a say in our new book ideas and help us publish the best in women's fiction

In addition, you will have a chance to win great prizes and receive special gifts!
See Web site for details. Some conditions apply.
Space is limited.

To join, visit us at
www.TellHarlequin.com.

REQUEST YOUR FREE BOOKS!

2 FREE NOVELS PLUS 2 FREE GIFTS!

▼ Silhouette®

SPECIAL EDITION®

Life, Love and Family!

YES! Please send me 2 FREE Silhouette Special Edition® novels and my 2 FREE gifts (gifts are worth about $10). After receiving them, if I don't wish to receive any more books, I can return the shipping statement marked "cancel." If I don't cancel, I will receive 6 brand-new novels every month and be billed just $4.24 per book in the U.S. or $4.99 per book in Canada. That's a savings of at least 15% off the cover price! It's quite a bargain! Shipping and handling is just 50¢ per book.* I understand that accepting the 2 free books and gifts places me under no obligation to buy anything. I can always return a shipment and cancel at any time. Even if I never buy another book from Silhouette, the two free books and gifts are mine to keep forever.

235 SDN EYN4 335 SDN EYPG

Name	(PLEASE PRINT)
Address	Apt. #
City	State/Prov.	Zip/Postal Code

Signature (if under 18, a parent or guardian must sign)

Mail to the Silhouette Reader Service:
IN U.S.A.: P.O. Box 1867, Buffalo, NY 14240-1867
IN CANADA: P.O. Box 609, Fort Erie, Ontario L2A 5X3

Not valid to current subscribers of Silhouette Special Edition books.

Want to try two free books from another line?
Call 1-800-873-8635 or visit www.morefreebooks.com.

* Terms and prices subject to change without notice. Prices do not include applicable taxes. Sales tax applicable in N.Y. Canadian residents will be charged applicable provincial taxes and GST. Offer not valid in Quebec. This offer is limited to one order per household. All orders subject to approval. Credit or debit balances in a customer's account(s) may be offset by any other outstanding balance owed by or to the customer. Please allow 4 to 6 weeks for delivery. Offer available while quantities last.

Your Privacy: Silhouette is committed to protecting your privacy. Our Privacy Policy is available online at www.eHarlequin.com or upon request from the Reader Service. From time to time we make our lists of customers available to reputable third parties who may have a product or service of interest to you. If you would prefer we not share your name and address, please check here. ☐

SSE09R

COMING NEXT MONTH

Available June 30, 2009

SPECIAL EDITION

#1981 THE TEXAS BILLIONAIRE'S BRIDE—Crystal Green
The Foleys and the McCords
For Vegas showgirl turned nanny Melanie Grandy, caring for the daughter of gruff billionaire Zane Foley was the perfect gig…until she fell for him, and her secret past threatened to bring down the curtain on her newfound happiness.

#1982 THE DOCTOR'S SECRET BABY—Teresa Southwick
Men of Mercy Medical
It was no secret that Emily Summers had shared a night of passion with commitment-phobe Dr. Cal Westen. But she kept him in the dark when she had their child. Would a crisis bring them together as a family…for good?

#1983 THE 39-YEAR-OLD VIRGIN—Marie Ferrarella
It wasn't easy when Claire Santaniello had to leave the convent to teach and take care of her sick mother. Luckily, widowed father and vice detective Caleb McClain was there for her as she found her way in the world…and into his arms.

#1984 HIS BROTHER'S BRIDE-TO-BE—Patricia Kay
Jill Jordan Emerson was engaged to a wealthy businessman several years her senior—until she came face-to-face with his younger brother Stephen Wells, a.k.a. the long-lost father of her son! Now which brother would claim this bride-to-be as his own?

#1985 LONE STAR DADDY—Stella Bagwell
Men of the West
It was a simple case of illegal cattle trafficking on a New Mexico ranch, and Ranger Jonas Redman thought he had the assignment under control—until the ranch's very single, very pregnant heiress Alexa Cantrell captured his attention and wouldn't let go….

#1986 YOUR RANCH OR MINE?—Cindy Kirk
Meet Me in Montana
When designer Anna Anderssen came home to Sweet River, she should have known she'd run right into neighboring rancher Mitchell Donovan, the one man who could expose the secrets—and reignite passions—that made her run in the first place!